MW01136734

Rosa Mistika

EUPHRASE KEZILAHABI

Rosa
Mistika

A NOVEL

*Translated from the Swahili by
Jay Boss Rubin*

Foreword by Annmarie Drury

A MARGELLOS
WORLD REPUBLIC OF LETTERS BOOK

Yale UNIVERSITY PRESS | NEW HAVEN & LONDON

Published with assistance from the Mary Cady Tew Memorial Fund.

The Margellos World Republic of Letters is dedicated to making literary works from around the globe available in English through translation. It brings to the English-speaking world the work of leading poets, novelists, essayists, philosophers, and playwrights from Europe, Latin America, Africa, Asia, and the Middle East to stimulate international discourse and creative exchange.

English translation copyright © 2025 by Jay Boss Rubin. Foreword copyright © 2025 by Annmarie Drury.
Originally published as *Rosa Mistika,* copyright © Euphrase Kezilahabi (East African Literature Bureau, 1971; second edition Dar es Salaam University Press, 1988).

This book may not be reproduced, in whole or in part, including illustrations, in any form (beyond that copying permitted by Sections 107 and 108 of the U.S. Copyright Law and except by reviewers for the public press), without written permission from the publishers.

Yale University Press books may be purchased in quantity for educational, business, or promotional use. For information, please email sales.press@yale.edu (U.S. office) or sales@yaleup.co.uk (U.K. office).

Set in Source Serif type by Motto Publishing Services.
Printed in the United States of America.

Library of Congress Control Number: 2024950803
ISBN 978-0-300-27655-8 (paperback)

A catalogue record for this book is available from the British Library.

Authorized Representative in the EU: Easy Access System Europe, Mustamäe tee 50, 10621 Tallinn, Estonia, gpsr.requests@easproject.com

10 9 8 7 6 5 4 3 2 1

I give thanks to my dear mentors:
Pauline Magere and Vedastus M. Machumu,
for pushing me into the ocean
so I'd start to swim like an ant.

*   *   *

For Mama Edna Bilenjo:
How can a person ever thank their mother
enough for the kindness she showed them
when they were still a little child?

Contents

Foreword

by Annmarie Drury

First published in 1971 and regarded as a foundational work of modern Swahili literature, *Rosa Mistika* is often described as a novel of social realism. It is an apt description: the novel captures many elements of Tanzanian life in the years immediately following independence. The role of the Development Officer ("Bwana Maendeleo" in Swahili), the clandestine distillery of chapter 7, the criticism by a police officer of the drinkers there, who are "ruining this country for the rest of us" (p. 58), and the dance hall scenes that Kezilahabi renders with relish, from the moment when "the record is placed on the turntable and the speakers start to shake with sound" (p. 46)—all these belong to young, postcolonial Tanzania. The novel indeed delivers much of its social critique in a realist mode. As it explores parenting, for instance, and pursues an underlying question about what the new country of Tanzania needs to flourish, the novel highlights a need to wrestle with what it means to parent well, to recognize how much good parenting matters to the task of building a good society. There are moments when Rosa seems to express the author's thoughts on the subject: "'Oh, Charles,' Rosa sighed, 'if parents could only understand that a single action of theirs can destroy their children's lives, they'd grasp the weight of their authority and be more careful'" (p. 115). And there are moments when the narrative seems to channel an authorial perspective in other terms: "Let us agree, finally, that the days of locking our daughters inside and anointing them with oil are over. Ours is not a world to be told about, as in 'The world is like this and like that.' Ours is a world to go out into, as in *see, decide, act*" (p. 70). The idea that each person must venture out and "see, decide, act" is very Kezilahabian, and *Rosa Mistika* insists that it is a need for all young people regardless of gender—that it is a human need.

This need to see and decide for oneself applies to the reader, too. It is part of Kezilahabi's artistic ethos. Thus, there are moments when the narrative voice presents Rosa through the lens of a blinkered and unsympathetic conventional morality. These passages can be uncomfortable to read, and I cannot think that Kezilahabi intended them to be otherwise. Similarly, the novel's critiques of Rosa's father, Zakaria, are trenchant, yet its late sections approach him from another angle, describing him as a village jester: "According to the customs of the Wakerewe, a jester can jest at any time and in any place other than a court of law. A jester can also take from his jestees anything not exceeding one goat in value. The jestee must not get angry at this, either. This was how Zakaria pointed out to his neighbors the absurdities of their common existence" (p. 135). In this way we experience the novel's investigation into character and Kezilahabi's experiment with it. To propose to know everything would perhaps be the greatest danger. People, too, are puzzles—*mafumbo,* to use a pertinent Swahili word—and a sense of the mystery of human agency and motivation informs the novel.

But social realism describes the novel only in part. It contains layers and surprises, shifting as it does between narrative approaches. There is a surreal courtroom scene with God as judge; there are anthropological modes of narration in a late exploration of Zakaria in the village; and there are intentionally didactic passages resembling oral storytelling. A reader can find elements of melodrama, parable, and song. Kezilahabi's interest in synthesizing art forms from across cultures, an interest that animates his entire body of work, is vividly present here. Through variation in narrative mode and voice, the novel shows us new dimensions of Rosa's world, sometimes undoing earlier certainties.

Kezilahabi came by his identity as synthesizer and comparatist naturally. Well versed in multiple languages and cultural traditions, he could scarcely have been otherwise, as was evident even in casual conversation. He once described to me, with rueful approval, how many different forms of greeting there are in Kikerewe, depending on one's age, relation to the greeting's recipient, and more—so many that one might be hesitant to venture to say hello at all! Yet he explored the creative powers of cultural synthesis with uncommon intelligence, originality, and verve, and *Rosa Mistika* marks an early milestone in that dimension of his life's work.

In one of the novel's most peaceful instants, we learn that Rosa is a reader. She is home from school, and as domestic life proceeds around her, she reads a novel. It is the novel *Kusadikika,* a late, speculative fiction by the great Swahili writer Shaaban Robert, who anticipated but did not live to see Tanzania's independence. *Kusadikika* offers a veiled critique of colonialism and a nudge toward the possibility of a different kind of governance. As Rosa reads Shaaban Robert,

Kezilahabi suggests his—and Rosa's—affiliation with authors who try to envision a better world. Is it possible to bring about a more just society through reading and writing? What resources can literature offer to the task of nation building? The personal and the social, family and country: How can we think about these categories together? Kezilahabi's fiction suggests his strong conviction that asking such questions and thinking critically about their answers contribute to the common good.

In his own life, Kezilahabi journeyed far from his beginning—shared with the titular character of this novel, Rosa—on the Tanzanian island of Ukerewe, in Lake Victoria, and Ukerewe had enduring importance to his art. After early schooling near his home, he studied at a Catholic secondary school in the port city of Mwanza before continuing his education at the University of Dar es Salaam. In the early 1970s, he worked as a secondary school teacher. He later worked at the University of Dar es Salaam, studied in Wisconsin, returned to the University of Dar es Salaam, and taught at the University of Botswana. As he moved from place to place and spent time in many different classrooms as teacher and as learner, Kezilahabi had opportunity to ponder forms of knowledge and approaches to sharing it, and he did so extensively, across his life. Yet *Rosa Mistika,* his first novel, published when he was in his mid-twenties, sits closest to the heart of his own experiences as a youthful learner and teacher.

A sense of Kezilahabi's familiarity with the world of schooling emerges at many moments in *Rosa Mistika,* as when the new head of Rosa's teacher training college, Bwana Albert, settles in to work at home in the evening: "He was serious, hardworking; the storm didn't frighten him. After he closed the windows, he returned to the task of sorting class schedules. Like a boy holding on to a special promise, Albert felt no fatigue. He kept on working while he cooked his dinner" (p. 101). The small pleasure of "two sodas and a loaf of bread from the cupboard" (p. 101) that Albert begins to enjoy is soon postponed. In these moments, a reader senses that Kezilahabi knows well the routines of a young administrator like Bwana Albert and sympathizes with him, even while preparing narratively to upend his staid evening of work.

Letters were important for Kezilahabi, who once told me about the thrill of receiving, while teaching at a secondary school, a letter inviting him to take up a position at the University of Dar es Salaam. Letters also have a central role in the plot of *Rosa Mistika*. Early in the novel, a tenderly written letter causes uproar in the household of fifteen-year-old Rosa, giving readers a chance to witness Rosa's adamance and her profound vulnerability. Soon, a letter of acceptance from secondary school offers Rosa an imperfect avenue of escape. Rosa writes letters home. Young men write letters to her. Anonymously written letters upset characters' lives. And in a poignant moment, Rosa throws away an arduously written letter sent by her mother. Kezilahabi crafts the content of this letter with care, so that errors in spelling and grammar suggest the challenge that writing it entailed for Rosa's mother. He lingers on the story of its composition: "Her mother, who had in fact just taken an adult literacy class that met under a tree, put a great deal of effort into writing Rosa the letter. She spent a very long time composing it" (p. 69). This letter from home emblematizes the maternal love that is one of the novel's central themes—and perhaps one of the few things it celebrates unequivocally. When Rosa casually throws away her mother's missive, the novel shows us a difficult truth: negotiating origins can be hard, and sometimes one is not ready to hear from home. It would be easy to imagine (though the narrative does not tell us this) that Rosa's mother, Regina, would comprehend Rosa's action, for as the narrator tells us in introducing her, "She understood. Regina understood" (p. 4).

When I think about letters in *Rosa Mistika,* I also think about how, as a mentor, Kezilahabi showed me kindness through letters. A letter of support he wrote to help me go to Tanzania for the first time, to research a literary debate, still sits in a wallet on my bookshelf. Throughout the year I pursued that research in Tanzania, I carried it like a passport, certain that word from him could assist a traveler there in foreseeable and unforeseeable ways. By the time I reached Dar es Salaam, Kezilahabi had moved to Gaborone to take up a position at the University of Botswana, as he explained to me in another letter; but his colleagues in Dar es Salaam would assist me, that letter promised, and so they did. Years later, when I had an opportunity to go to Gaborone and Kezilahabi generously invited me to stay with his family, I again benefited from a commitment to assisting learners and artists that Kezilahabi demonstrated across his life. He had written to me in advance—by email, now—to describe the shirt he would be wearing when he met me in the Gaborone airport, so that I could easily find him. Though my flight was nearly six hours late, there he stood, in the very shirt, and drove me home to his family. Generous with his time, he always kept his word.

When I first read *Rosa Mistika* years ago, the unfamiliar language, the unsettling narration of sexual experience, and the stunning hardships in Rosa's life preoccupied me. Now I think also about the novel's historical context and how its narrative both represents and challenges the culture from which it emerged. In Tanzania in the early 1970s, it was unusual for a Swahili novel to feature a girl protagonist, and it was controversial for an author to represent the sexual experiences of a young woman, particularly abortion and sexual violence. *Rosa Mistika* was banned for years in Tanzanian schools (where it later became part of the curriculum), but provocation—through content, form, style—was for Kezilahabi an artist's duty. A young man himself when writing *Rosa,* he sympathized deeply with Tanzanian youth, and the novel brings to light problems that bedeviled young people: violence against girls and women at home, sexual exploitation of schoolgirls away from home, a sexual morality dominated by idealization of feminine purity and denial of women's sexual experience, the role of powerful men in enabling and perpetuating exploitation of young women, and the difficulty of talking about sexual politics. The resilience of women as they face domestic hardship is a key theme of the book. This novel describes the rhythm of days—the coming and going to the fields, to school, to shops; the cows that Regina cares for; the boys who show up pretending to be buying eggs when really they hope to see Rosa. Farming is central to the household economy, and Kezilahabi's knowledge of the work of the fields vivifies the novel's account of

Regina's acumen and devotion to her children. Here, Regina strategizes to find money for Rosa's school fees:

> The one cow that remained couldn't be sold because it was no longer calving. Not only that; Rosa's younger sisters' school fees were due, too. Regina still had her cassava fields—three or four acres of them. She told Rosa to harvest one acre. Her sisters volunteered to help. The work took a long time. Digging up the cassava, removing its bark-like peel, sun-curing it and preparing it for sale—none of these tasks was easy. Three weeks passed; the cassava chips were ready to sell. The pile sat in front of their house for two days, no customers to be found. (p. 28)

This attention to domestic life illuminates the inequalities and violence experienced by Regina and her daughters. They suffer from the brutality of Zakaria and from his drinking and negligence—and it is they who must work hard to cultivate and harvest and Regina who must somehow make ends meet so Rosa can continue to study. In representing these many dimensions of Rosa's world and adopting an array of narrative approaches, Kezilahabi yet holds his fundamental task steadily in view. To spell out the thinking of characters having difficult, unpleasant, or morally mistaken thoughts, to inquire into the interior lives and moral universes underlying everyday exchanges between men and women, to try to understand—and, above all, to want something better for Rosa: all this is the novel's project.

It has been a privilege to witness the development of this translation of an author whose work and generous friendship mean and meant very much to me. When I first read Jay

Boss Rubin's translation of *Rosa Mistika,* I was startled in the opening sentences by hearing a writerly voice I had known only in Swahili, that of the *Rosa Mistika* narrator, and something of a human voice I had known in real life—the inflection of Kezilahabi—brought into an English *Rosa*. What a discovery that was. I remain deeply admiring of how Jay Boss Rubin found for the novel an English that animates its story and the thinking of its author. I hope readers will find in it the absorbing reading experience that Rosa, under her tree, enjoys with the copy of Shaaban Robert that Kezilahabi gives to her.

Part One

Chapter 1

In Lake Victoria—as it's known today—there's an island about thirty miles from Mwanza called Ukerewe. When there's no fog, you can see it all the way from shore. In the middle of the island, a large structure built by the Germans is still standing. Nearby is a hanging tree—the tree that was used to hang Black people, I mean. The old colonial-era building marks the center of Namagondo. Not far away lived a woman named Regina.

Regina was known throughout the village. If you saw her walking, you'd think she was afraid of poking holes in God's earth; but if you asked her, she'd say, "I'm scared to crush any of God's creatures." She had a habit of licking her fingers while eating. When her children teased her about it, she told them, "My babes, you weren't alive yet at the time of the last famine. We ate tree roots. A person could be bought for one jerry can of millet!" But ever since she'd been married, she hadn't been well: she was troubled and tortured by her husband for a mistake she didn't make.

In the entire village of Namagondo, Regina was the only woman who was beaten practically every week. Many women in the village asked themselves why she didn't want to leave her husband. Some felt pity for her; more, though, felt she was a fool.

Regina had five children, all daughters, all of them pretty like their mother. Her hopes of continuing to live with them, her husband had told her, rested on her carrying to term her pregnancy that was currently in its fifth month. Regina hadn't needed to be told this, let alone reminded of it. She understood. Regina understood: she took care not to sleep on her stomach, she abstained from fish with small bones, she avoided carrying heavy loads. She was terrified of having a miscarriage. It wasn't the pregnancy alone that made Regina not leave her husband; it was also the love she had for her children. She didn't want to be apart from them; without her, her husband would be unable to care for them. All her thoughts revolved around her children's future happiness.

Thoughts such as these were circling through Regina's head when she heard a voice in the distance: "Hoi! Hoi! Hoi!" She understood. Regina understood who it was and what kind of condition they were in: it was a voice she had long been familiar with. Right away, she hurried her children to bed. The voice grew closer, and now Regina could make out the words being said.

"Every day I find them there—every day! I've already told them that all the wizards in Namagondo put together couldn't best me, but do they listen?" The voice was just outside the house now. The children cowered under the covers, quiet as could be.

"Regina! Open the door."

Regina got up slowly and went to open it.

"The wizards tried to kill me again just now, over by the road, but I chased them away! ALL of them! Didn't you hear them running?"

Regina didn't respond.

"Where are my children?" asked Zakaria.

"They've gone to bed," Regina answered, with as much deference as she could muster.

"What kind of wife are you? Answering me rudely like that. Wake them up," he said. "I want to see them."

With sadness but without complaint, Regina went to the children's room. She was afraid of getting hit. Among Regina's children, Rosa Mistika, or Rosa, for short, was the first-born. Rosa was a good-looking girl, on the tall side, humble and not too talkative. When she went to the spring to bathe, you could see her looking this way and that before taking off her clothes. Then she'd undress and bathe in a hurry before throwing her clothes back on, collecting water and heading home. When she arrived home, she often found that she still had soap bubbles in her ears. She didn't like to be stared at. If you looked her in the eye, she'd lower her head. Rosa was fifteen years old and in Standard Seven.

When Flora went to the spring, she would admire herself for a long, long time before beginning to bathe. She stared at her breasts, which were now large; she ran her hands down her back to the folds of her buttocks, then moved on to her chest and stroked down to the curve of her stomach; then she admired herself all over again. After bathing, she'd wait until the sun dried her skin before she put her clothes back on. If she went to the spring at two in the afternoon, she'd return home, bathing stone in hand, at five in the evening, even though the spring was only a mile away. Every time, her mother cursed her for being lazy. If Regina told Flora to go work on the family farm, Flora would pick up a younger sibling and set them on her hip. If told to light a cooking fire, Flora would pull dried grass from the roof of the kitchen instead of gathering kindling from the yard.

Honorata came after Flora. Honorata tended her own

cotton field. She loved to work. Oftentimes, you could hear her crying for her hoe. Although she was pretty, it was as if she didn't realize it: she wore any old clothes and didn't care about putting oil in her hair. "Water's good enough," she would say. Nine years old and in Standard Three, that was Honorata.

Stella followed Honorata. If you stopped by to say hello, you might find her sitting on the ground with her legs splayed apart. If her mother were to say, "Ah, ah, Stella!" Stella would correct her posture and laugh, then toss her legs open again as soon as Regina turned her back. When visitors came, she climbed on their backs. One day, she used a guest's walking stick to wipe chicken shit off the bottom of her foot. But whenever her mother made the mistake of disciplining her with a slap, Stella would refuse to eat all day, until she was nuzzled and coddled. Twice already, she had fallen from trees. Her clothes often ripped right down the middle. You could see Stella holding the flaps of her clothes together while she ran so her stomach wouldn't be visible. That was Stella, apple of her father's eye.

Sperantia didn't yet know how to talk. If you asked her, "Do you want some candy?" she'd answer, "Yep." If you asked her, "Do you want to get hit?" she'd say the same thing. One day she was stung by a scorpion, and Regina couldn't figure out where on her body to apply the medicine. Sperantia pointed to her head then pointed to her arms, then pointed to her feet.

As Zakaria entered the house, the girls pretended to be asleep, but they heard every word their father said. Because Rosa had already started menstruating, she was left alone. Flora, who was in Standard Five, was forced to get up, along with Honorata and Stella. As soon as they were brought before their father, Zakaria started up with his usual antics.

"Okay, wipe the sleep from your eyes! Fa-all in! About fa-ace!" he began. "About fa-ace!" he said again. "Ten-hut! At ease!" Then he instructed them to mark time: "Left, right, left, right! Arms up! Arms down! Up! Down!"

"I'm tired," Stella said; the others laughed at her.

"Okay, now sing!" Zakaria commanded his daughters. He cued them up: "*Off they went on a hunt one day . . .*"

The girls all fell in line and began to sing:

Off they went on a hunt one day, to the forest they did go.
When they saw old Rabbit, they chased him down with hounds.
Rabbit ran away so fast, he ducked down in his hole.
In his hole he sung his song, his very sad, sad song:
I never tasted calabash, never made it to the farm.
What mistake did I make, to get chased down by hounds?

"Again!" Zakaria ordered. The children started from the top.

Many years earlier, Zakaria had been a schoolteacher, but he was dismissed for drunkenness. His neighbors said that he cared more about booze than children: he hadn't shelled out a single banknote for his own kids' school fees. That they were in school at all was thanks to their mother—hats off to Regina. She put significant energy into her cotton-growing operation, and with the money that she earned she put clothes on her children's backs. But the one thing that really enabled Regina to pay for her children's educations? Cattle. Regina inherited four cows from her father after he passed. In order to make ends meet, she'd already had to sell two of them. Meanwhile, Zakaria hadn't even managed to put a proper roof over their heads. Night after night, stars shone down on them through the holes in the ceiling. From Friday to Sunday, Zakaria went out drinking, and the other days of the week he stayed in bed and pretended to be sick. His wife couldn't figure out how many shillings he had in the bank, yet she took note of his weekly binges.

While his children sang, Zakaria danced—he jumped side to side, back and forth. Maybe everything would've gone okay if Stella hadn't started blathering. She couldn't keep a secret, perhaps because she was still so young. Twice already, Regina had been beaten as a result of Stella's chattering. On two separate occasions, Stella had announced that a man had come to call on her mother. They had only been traveling salesmen, but in Zakaria's eyes, Stella revealed hidden truths. That's why he loved her as much as he did.

"Baba, Baba," Stella called to Zakaria.

"Mm," he responded.

"Todaay! Todaay! Rosa she—she got a letter," she blurted out. "A letter along with twenty shillings. She showed us and everything."

Zakaria turned ugly the moment he heard the news. Rosa was summoned. She entered the room, her bedsheet trailing behind her. Before she could say even a word, the blow landed and she fell to the ground. Rosa tried to get up and run away, but the sheet tangled her feet and knocked her down again. She was at the mercy of her father.

"Bring me the letter! Where is it? Bring it along with the money you were given. You think we're in need of charity, is that it?"

Rosa was struck again and again, open-handed slaps one after another until blood flowed from her mouth and nose. "Baba, have mercy on me!" Rosa cried. "It won't happen again. I promise!" The sheet disappeared, snatched away. Only her underwear saved her from being completely exposed—woe unto those who gaze upon their grown daughter's breasts! Regina started to wail. Tears cascaded down her cheeks. As soon as the children saw their mother crying, they started crying as well. Total uproar ensued. Even Stella was crying. Zakaria didn't care; he grabbed his walking stick and roared at his eldest daughter as he chased her into the bedroom she shared with her sisters.

"You must show me the letter!" he yelled at Rosa. "You want to follow in the whorish path of your mother, is that it?"

Humiliated, Rosa retrieved her book bag. She withdrew the letter from her geography notebook, along with five shillings. She handed the money over to her father; the letter she crumpled up and tossed in her mouth. She tried to chew it, but her father grabbed her throat. Rosa didn't spit it out. Zakaria squeezed harder. Rosa's eyes began to turn red, her tongue hung out of her mouth, and then the letter dropped to the floor. It was slippery, like a hen puked up by a python. Zakaria picked it up right away.

"Who gave you this letter? Say his name," he commanded.

With great difficulty Rosa uttered, "Charles."

Charles was a skinny kijana, a little on the tall side, with light skin and a very handsome face. At that time, he was being raised by his uncle Ndalo, so he could go to school. When he passed the exam at the end of Standard Four, he was selected to attend Murutunguru Upper Primary School.

Because he lived in Itira, around seven miles away, he was obliged to move somewhere closer. On the day he arrived at his uncle's place, he found Rosa paying a visit to Bigeyo, Charles's aunt and Ndalo's wife. Charles was introduced to Rosa, and Rosa to Charles. That's how they learned that they'd be classmates. Because Ndalo and Bigeyo hadn't been blessed with children of their own, they cared for Charles as if he were their son.

Every morning, Charles waited for Rosa so they could walk to school together. Afternoons, they accompanied each other home. Zakaria had never said a word about it because he saw his daughter as still very young. Two years had already passed in this manner. After three years of daily walks, they were in Standard Seven, and the path they had traveled had caused them to fall in love. Neither, however, was brave enough to share their feelings with the other. Finally, Charles recognized that his stay at his aunt and uncle's place was coming to an end; he summoned the courage to compose the letter.

If the wind hadn't been blowing to the west that night, Charles and his aunt and uncle would have heard the screams; it was only a quarter mile from Ndalo's to Zakaria's. Charles had already retired to his single-room grass hut. He was reading *Kiongozi,* the weekly Catholic newspaper, when he heard someone calling. He opened the door and stepped outside, dressed in a sheet of his own. In the center of the compound, Zakaria stood next to his daughter, gripping a spear. Rosa was still shedding tears. Ndalo and Bigeyo came out into the yard wrapped in bedsheets, too. Lo! The moon and stars shone down on them. They looked like angels sent from heaven to witness earthly cruelty—not only between

human and human, but between father and daughter. Zakaria began to speak in a loud voice:

"Charles! From this day forward, you will cease to walk
with my daughter. Take your measly shillings!" he said as he
threw the paper currency at Charles. "You think we're poor?
That we're unable to work for a living, that we don't have
hands?"

With that, he grabbed Rosa by the back of the neck, pull-
ing the collar of her dress tight, and began pushing her
home. When they arrived, Rosa saw that Regina had already
heated water to soothe the wounds on her face, and so Rosa
could clean the blood out of her mouth. After her mother
washed her, Rosa went and lay down. She cried nearly the
whole night through.

Zakaria uncrumpled the letter as soon as he got to his
room. He took it in. With great difficulty, he read:

Namagondo,
P.O. Box Lover's Lane,
Ukerewe

To my lover Rosa Mistika,

You, you mysterious rose, you! You, my comfort-giving sister
from just down the way! Open your eyes to this brief declaration of
love. Every night I dream of you; when I'm not dreaming of you,
I lie awake thinking of you. I can't bear it any longer. Answer me
quickly, please. I wish you great success in passing your test!

Yours in hope and in love,
Charles Lusato

Zakaria turned off the light and drowsiness overtook him. The wind blew in gently through the window and spread through the house. Zakaria heard it whistling in his ears as he climbed under the covers. It was as if the wind had entered to say, *Amani duniani kwa watu wenye malezi mema.*

Peace on earth to all those with good upbringing.

Chapter 2

This was the manner in which Rosa was brought up; this was the manner in which she was cared for; this was the manner in which she was watched over by her father. After the beating, Rosa ceased talking to boys altogether. When Zakaria learned of this, he was very happy. He boasted—especially when he'd had a little to drink—that he knew how to raise his daughters. But Zakaria didn't understand that Rosa was at a difficult age, and that strictness was not appropriate; he didn't understand that daughters require a certain independence from their fathers; he didn't understand that by beating his daughter, he was exercising an authority he didn't rightfully possess, and that when it came to opinions on marriage, his were practically worthless. He didn't understand that Rosa needed to get to know boys. And so, as a result of her upbringing, Rosa began to see boys as people she need not associate with, or even speak to. She began to think that she needed to be self-sufficient. Rosa grew more remote by the day.

Rosa's heart hardened with ideas such as these in isolation; Charles had already gone home to Itira. One day, Rosa got word that the results of their end-of-year exam had been posted at school. She heard that Charles had passed and would be headed to Mkwawa. She had been selected to go to Rosary, a girls' school. Because secondary school tuition was paid by the government, Rosa sensed a possible path forward. But things weren't as simple as she hoped. After a few days, Rosa received her official acceptance letter from Rosary. The letter didn't just mention her accomplishment: it instructed her to arrive at the school with thirty shillings for her uniform, plus shoes, bedding, and a sturdy trunk. And money for toiletries, on top of all that? The path forward seemed untenable.

Zakaria claimed he had nothing to contribute. So a plan was made to sell one of the family's two remaining cattle. Regina didn't object; it was still her intention to further her daughters' educations. When Zakaria went off to drink that day, he spread the news that he had a cow for sale.

Two days later, two young men arrived from the town of Nansio. They were fortunate to find both Zakaria and Regina at home. The starting price for the cow was 250 shillings, but after the young men argued that the cow had tapeworms, the price dropped to 180. The cow was sold. Now only one cow remained. As the young men left with their purchase, Stella started to scream.

"Thieves! Leave my cow alone!" She picked up the rope fastened to the cow's horn and pulled, and the cow started to return. Regina grabbed hold of Stella; the young men left with the cow. Stella threw herself to the ground and rolled about as she cried in vain; all in vain.

Rosa was given seventy shillings to purchase her trunk, bedding, and shoes. The other 110 shillings Regina set aside for Rosa in her jewelry box until the day of her departure. Rosa was elated.

That evening around four o'clock, Regina had just finished digging up potatoes, and Zakaria was beginning to
gather pieces of old cloth from around the house, dark-
colored scraps his wife had no more use for. Zakaria was a
person with a real sense of humor; but sometimes his jokes
went a little too far. Although he was quite strict when it
came to parenting, he was still capable of laughing and ex-
periencing happiness along with his family. He started tearing the cloth into long strips and twisting them together into
a large rope.

He was almost finished when Stella scooted up to him
and started asking questions.

"What are you going to do with that rope?" she asked, her
hand on her chin.

"Ooh," he answered. "I want to go and recover that cow
of ours."

"When will you come back?" asked Stella.

"Tonight."

"But why are you making a rope out of old clothes? Why
aren't you using sisal thread?" Zakaria smiled a little, realiz-
ing his child wanted insight into his craftiness.

"Ooh," he said. "I want to steal our cow back after it's
dark; a rope of dark material will be less visible. . . . Here,
hold this end of the rope," he instructed. "Now pull!" Stella
pulled, but Zakaria's pull in the opposite direction nearly
toppled her over.

"Pull hard," Zakaria said.

Stella pulled again.

"Okay, good."

The rope was ready and Zakaria left for Nansio, walking
stick in hand, laughing to himself. Regina returned home as

evening fell, and right away Stella reported that Zakaria had gone to recover their cow. Regina understood what he was really up to. While he was at home, at least, Zakaria rarely said explicitly that he was going out to drink.

The sun set and darkness spread. Regina's daughters loaded firewood into the stove so it was ready for cooking. That night, it was Flora's turn to stir the ugali. Just as the water started to boil and was ready for the flour to be added, Honorata began to shove Flora, trying to get Flora to move from the cooking stool so she could take over. Regina pushed Honorata away and she fell to the floor. She wouldn't have gotten so angry if Stella hadn't made a face at her, balled up her fingers into a fist, and sneered, "Woo!" Honorata jumped toward Stella and gave her a kick. Stella cried out in pain.

Regina reached for her stick, but Honorata dashed outside before she could use it. Regina couldn't run after her. Flora had already dished up the ugali. Regina complimented her on a job well done and told her she would make some man a lucky husband someday. Zakaria's portion was set off to the side. When it came time to eat, Regina called to Honorata. She told her to come back to the kitchen and forget about her misdeeds. She even broke her stick into little pieces and tossed them outside. Honorata returned. They all knelt in a circle with their toes pointed back behind them; Regina kept an eye on the ugali over her shoulder. When she extended her legs forward, Sperantia came and sat on top of them without being told what to do.

Regina used mealtimes to educate and admonish her daughters. Tonight, she began with Stella. "If you don't stop your lying, I'll cut out your tongue and cut off your ears!" The others laughed. Stella pouted. Regina reminded Stella to bow to the ground every time she fetched something for her father. She reminded Honorata that, whenever she saw a visitor approaching their compound, she was to take the visitor's walking stick for them, and to offer them a chair at once. Flora was scolded for her lazy farm work: the other day, Honorata had finished tending two rows of crops while Flora hadn't finished even one.

Because Rosa was already a young woman, at least in the biological sense, the remarks Regina offered to her went like this: "My child, you have now become an adult. Soon you'll travel across the channel to the land of the Sukuma people. Don't forget about your parents over there—we should write to each other as often as possible. There is one matter in particular I would like to caution you about before you go: rude, reckless boys. Boys are going to proposition you and try to get you pregnant, and any pregnancy will cut short your ability to stay in school. Avoid these boys at all costs. But if you happen to act like a fool and end up pregnant, don't abort it. More and more, I'm hearing about girls who are getting abortions so they can continue with their studies. They love their studies more than children. Even so, it's murder."

Regina paused for a moment and drank some water. Then she continued: "Children come about by the grace of God. Not everyone gets to have one. See how Bigeyo is suffering. So—in the same manner I gave birth to you—if you get pregnant, you should drop out of school; keep the pregnancy. If you're afraid about raising the child, don't worry, I'll help. All the schoolgirls who are getting abortions will be sorry someday; they'll be surprised to find out, later on, that they aren't getting pregnant anymore. When they're still schoolgirls, they don't see the advantage in having a child.

When they're old, walking with canes, they'll cry out for their children that they killed back when they were school-girls! People say this country is getting too crowded. I don't see how that can be a justification for killing a child who has already entered the womb."

Regina was a wise woman, even without having under-gone any formal education. As she finished saying these words to Rosa, she saw Sperantia swaying back and forth with drowsiness. She told her children to hurry up and fin-ish eating, then get ready for bed. After they finished, they washed their hands in the metal pot before stacking the dishes to do in the morning. Honorata scooped up some veg-etables for Zakaria, and Regina set them aside along with his ugali. Flora picked up Sperantia, who was now asleep, and Rosa hoisted up her lamp so everyone could see where they were going. They exited the kitchen and headed toward the house to go to bed. When they arrived outside, Stella said, "What's that?" as she gazed up at the sky.

"It's a shooting star," Honorata answered.

Rosa told them that it was a rocket circling the earth. Soon, she added, America expected to land on the moon. Stella added that there's a rabbit on the moon; just the other day, she read it in a book.

Everyone went inside. Once in their bedroom, the girls tried to stump one another with riddles. When they tired of riddles, they began telling stories. The hour grew late. Hono-rata was in the middle of telling a tale; she stopped when she realized no one was listening. She went to extinguish the lamp and—lo!—she saw a big black snake slithering to-ward her from the rear door. She screamed at the top of her lungs, "Waayi!" The others jumped out of bed and began running to and fro, unaware of where the danger was. They all screamed and jammed against each other in the doorway. Eventually, everyone squeezed through. Stella was the last to pass. The snake grazed her foot, but it wasn't able to harm her. Regina had been fast asleep, but she was woken by the cries of her children. All her daughters were now in her room.

"Nyoka, nyoka!" Stella yelled. She continued: "It bit my foot!"

Since there wasn't a man in the house, Regina figured she had better defend herself and her children—or die trying. She grabbed the biggest stick she could find and headed toward the door. The snake was still crawling side to side; it looked as if it had gotten pinned in the doorway: it wasn't able to fully enter. Regina struck it twice—three times. Stella cheered her on: "Hit it! Hit it!" All of a sudden, the snake seemed to leap into the air. Regina threw her stick aside and ran. She came back with a spear and stabbed the snake in the head. By the time Stella counted to twelve, it appeared that the mysterious serpent was dead.

Regina had started to sweat. She was still wiping her brow when Zakaria shoved the door open and came in. Stella alerted him: "Nyoka! Make sure you don't step on it!" Zakaria laughed. He took the snake in his hands and held it up for Stella to see. Stella laughed so hard she cried. When the others realized what it was, they laughed until their ribs hurt.

The girls brought Zakaria his dinner. When he was done eating, he removed from his pocket a bottle of moonshine and started to drink. He gave his daughters some little sips so they could taste it, too. Zakaria finished just half the bottle, then went to sleep.

That night it rained and it poured. Lo! The house was like a tree. An astonishing amount of water poured in through the roof. Inside, there were a few cowhides scattered about. Regina took them and placed them over her children, and the drops of rain danced pata pata against the pelts.

Chapter 3

The days passed very slowly for Rosa. Then one day, as she was gazing at the calendar, her heart started to pound against her chest: she had never traveled by ferry before, she had never seen the city of Mwanza, had never seen three- or four-story buildings, had never seen a locomotive. When she was told how automobiles could cross over train tracks, she couldn't quite believe it. Finally, the day drew near; the calendar informed her she was to depart for secondary school the following Monday.

That Saturday, Rosa went to purchase her school supplies, accompanied by Flora. They went on foot—a distance of around six miles. Along the way, they crossed paths with some young men who tried to stop them. Rosa and Flora ran. Catcalls echoed behind them, but they didn't look back; they sped ahead like birds narrowly escaping from danger. Eventually they arrived in the town of Nansio and went into the Bata brand shoe store, where their neighbor Ndalo worked. They hoped he would help them select some good shoes for a nice price. They found a pair for Rosa to try on; she found that they fit.

"How much?" she inquired.

"Twenty-seven shillings," Ndalo answered, loud enough that the Indian shop owner would be sure to hear him.

"We don't have that much."

"How many shillings do you have?"

"We only have eighteen."

"That's it?" Ndalo said.

"That's all we have!" the girls answered in unison.

"Wait," Ndalo instructed. "I'll go ask the shop owner if there's anything we can do."

Ndalo went and consulted with the Indian man, who was sitting in his chair, chewing on something leafy.

"He says twenty-five is his final price," Ndalo reported back.

Rosa and Flora protested: "But we don't have that much!"

"They don't have it," Ndalo relayed to the shop owner.

"Nineteen shillings no hurt," the Indian man said.

"We said we don't have that much," the girls insisted.

"They don't have it," Ndalo repeated.

"Fine. Tell them check *all* other stores in area, then come back this one, eh?"

Ndalo told the girls, in the Kerewe language, to go try the store on the other side of the street. There, he said, they could get the same shoes for sixteen shillings.

The shop owner caught the switch and erupted into a fit. "Look, you, you ruin my bijiness!" he shouted. "Once I think you was hard worker. Really you just trickster, eh?" He pushed Ndalo out the door and threw his final five shillings of pay at Ndalo's chest.

"Take it! Go home and don't return! Go farm in the dirt!"

Ndalo was being abused as if his country had yet to gain independence. He began to unbutton his shirt.

"You baniani," he said, "I'm going to wreck you so badly that you'll no longer be able to taste your precious chili peppers!" Ndalo's shoulders bulged under his shirt. By the time he had taken it off, the Indian man had already run back inside and locked the door. Meanwhile, a crowd had gathered in the street.

"What a coward!" an onlooker said. Then, turning to Ndalo: "What, you can't throw a punch unless you're topless? Where in the world did you get that idea?" Ndalo tuned the man out along with the rest of the crowd. He put his shirt back on and set off toward home.

Rosa and Flora went into the shop across the street. They got the shoes for the very price Ndalo had told them they would. With the money left over, they bought Rosa's trunk and bedding. Because they had baggage now, they boarded a bus to return home. When they arrived, they found Bigeyo waiting for them; Rosa had asked her to come cut her hair.

They sat together in the shade of an orange tree. While Regina scrubbed Rosa's clothes, the scissors cried *kacha kacha kachu* over Rosa's head. Rosa kept looking at herself in the mirror, directing Bigeyo not to cut her hair too short in front. Stella saw something swoop out of the sky. She yelled and threw her hands in the air.

"Swa! Swa! Swa!"

The others, too, jumped up and began to shout, but it was no use. One chick was already swinging from the talons of the hawk. They were left to count the chicks that remained.

"There were ten. Now there are three!" Flora exclaimed. Rosa sat back down for her haircut. It wasn't long before the hawk returned. As it circled back, Honorata was the first to spot it.

"Swa! Swa! Swa!" She threw her hands in the air, "Swa!" The hawk had already snatched another chick. This time it didn't go far. It landed on a tree just outside the compound. The girls threw stones at it, but the stones fell short. The hawk ate the chick without a care in the world. When it was finished, it flew away delighted and full. Two chicks remained. It appeared that even the hawk knew that this was a women's compound.

The following morning, Rosa, Flora, and Honorata attended the early Mass in Murutunguru. Rosa wore her new shoes to the service, then carried them home in her hand. Back at the compound, they found Regina peeling potatoes. They could tell she was upset about something, so they looked for ways to help. They washed the potatoes and loaded them into the pot. Zakaria had gone off to worship at the altar of alcohol. People said that oftentimes after Zakaria purchased his booze, he'd raise his drinking bowl in the air and offer to those nearby: "Drink from this goblet, for it is my own true blood!" Zakaria loved a good joke.

On that day, Zakaria had passed by Ndalo's en route to his drinking club. When Rosa and Flora arrived home from Mass, they didn't find him there, but they could tell something was bothering their mother.

The rest of the day passed very, very slowly for Rosa. After lunch, she began ironing her clothes. When she was done with that, she packed up her things in her trunk. Rosa was struggling with her new lock when she heard her mother yelling and cursing at Stella.

"You mustn't take after your father's thieving!" Stella dodged two, three blows, then—whoosh!—off she ran to Bigeyo's. She'd been caught in the act, swiping a fish from the clay cooking pot. At sundown, Bigeyo brought Stella home and asked Regina for forgiveness on Stella's behalf. That night, Stella's words were few. She didn't even say anything during dinner. Regina looked at Rosa for a long time. She wanted to tell her what had happened. Regina hesitated: she felt pity for Rosa.

That night, Rosa didn't sleep. She got up and peered out the window. It was still dark. She tried closing her eyes. It was no use; slumber can't be forced. After a short while she got up again. It still wasn't light out. Sleep overtook her just before dawn. When she woke up the third time the birds had already begun to sing. Rosa looked out the window and couldn't believe her eyes. She saw two—no, three—men. The one in the middle was being carried, his toes brushing against the ground. She went to wake her mother the moment she realized it was her father.

"Hodi, hodi."

Regina opened the door.

"Where's his bed?" Ndalo asked. Zakaria was laid out on the bed. Ndalo explained that Zakaria had drunk a bottle and a half. When he showed them the bottle, it looked like Zakaria had drunk closer to two full bottles. Water was splashed on Zakaria's face, and he was brought milk to drink. He was given sips of lemon juice. At ten o'clock that morning, he was still out cold.

Rosa's trip was canceled, ruined. She couldn't go and leave her father like this. The entire afternoon, Zakaria's daughters orbited around him. They even ate their lunch at the foot of his bed. At six in the evening, Zakaria finally began to stir. He opened his eyes. Ndalo saw that he was going to be all right and went home. When Zakaria opened his eyes a second time, Regina asked him what she could bring him.

Zakaria was silent.

"What do you want to eat?" Regina asked, louder this time.

"Ooze, ooze," Zakaria answered in the faintest of voices.

They were afraid to bring him "ooze." They prepared uji for him instead. After a few spoonfuls of porridge, Zakaria was able to sit up in bed. When Ndalo came by that night to check on him, he found him still sitting up.

"Ah! Ah!" Zakaria began. "Yesterday's booze was enough to do us in. How many bottles did we drink again?"

"If I remember correctly, ten," Ndalo answered.

"U, u, u. Not even on Christmas do we drink like that!"

That night, Zakaria slept as he normally did. It seemed he had recovered. The following morning—by then it was Tuesday—Regina went to Ndalo's place on a fact-finding mission. As she approached, she was surprised to see what was transpiring there at the compound. Ndalo and Bigeyo were eating chicken meat while running around the outside of their house in circles.

Ndalo and Bigeyo were troubled by one matter in particular: having a child. They had already lost a great deal of money on fertility treatments. One year, they traveled to faraway lands and returned with half a jerry can of tree roots. The roots were gone, but there was no sign of a pregnancy. The following year they traveled elsewhere and met an mganga who told them that Bigeyo was infertile because, when she was a young girl, she refused to carry her younger siblings on her back. The necessary fertility treatment was to get her hands on a younger sibling's urine and pour it down her spine. But this wasn't going to be easy: her younger siblings were now all grown up.

After Ndalo and Bigeyo returned home, it wasn't long before one of Bigeyo's younger siblings paid her a visit. Bigeyo was thrilled. When it came time to go to bed, Bigeyo provided her younger sibling with a tin can. She told them that the village was riddled with wizards, that it was unsafe to venture outside during the night. Just pee in the can if you have to go, she told them. Early the next morning, Bigeyo took the can and poured its contents onto her back. Another year passed. Every time Bigeyo's stomach swelled from eating, Ndalo asked her if she'd gotten pregnant. Two years passed: there was no sign that Bigeyo had conceived.

The following year they tried going to the hospital. The doctor told them plainly that they weren't going to have a baby together, but they didn't believe it. Eventually they made the decision to travel into the north country; there they encountered another traditional healer. This one told them to eat the meat of a white-feathered hen while running around their house in circles in order to purify the compound. Regina had seen them eating meat in this manner. Whenever Bigeyo heard talk of all the schoolgirls getting abortions these days, she didn't believe it. "Yuuu! Yuuu!" she'd exclaim. "As for us," she'd say, hand on her face, "we must be cursed."

Regina would reply to her: "Schoolgirls these days treat pregnancies as if they were bed bugs. A person with bed bugs gets up, checks under the mattress, beneath the pillow, between the sheets, and in the corners of the bed until they find them and kill them.

"Schoolgirls these days are just as diligent when it comes to murdering their children. When they get pregnant, they think a bed bug has climbed into their stomach to suck their blood. They try as hard as they can to get it out. Schoolgirls get abortions like those women who fool around with men

on the side, then scare their children away when they're trying to follow them. 'Go home! If you come this way, you'll be
eaten by a genie!' And the child goes home running. Schoolgirls these days are no different," Regina would explain.
"They expel babies from their wombs so they can get back
to their business with other young people."

So it was that when Regina saw Ndalo and Bigeyo eating
chicken and running around in circles, she understood their
intention. She stood still for a while, waiting for them to
complete their deeds. When they were finished, she called
hodi at the entrance to their compound. Bigeyo told her all
about their latest mganga. After she finished relating her
tales from the north country, Regina asked the questions she
had come to ask. Ndalo told her, straight up, that the night
before Zakaria had been buying people drinks with abandon, that even those who didn't know him profited from his
generosity. He spent close to fifty shillings.

Regina walked home with her arms behind her back, like
a bereaved person. It was clear that Rosa wouldn't go to secondary school. Now Rosa understood. Her mother informed
her. Zakaria had forgotten to close her jewelry box after he
scooped out the money.

The one cow that remained couldn't be sold because it
was no longer calving. Not only that; Rosa's younger sisters' school fees were due, too. Regina still had her cassava
fields—three or four acres of them. She told Rosa to harvest
one acre. Her sisters volunteered to help. The work took a
long time. Digging up the cassava, removing its bark-like
peel, sun-curing it and preparing it for sale—none of these
tasks was easy. Three weeks passed; the cassava chips were
ready to sell. The pile sat in front of their house for two days,
no customers to be found. Rosa gave up hope.

Zakaria was at peace, as if these matters had nothing to do with him. He went on drinking his booze as usual. Regina hoped for customers every day. Eventually, an idea came into her head. She resolved to make a batch of cassava wine—mapuya, it's called. She got some millet in exchange for some cassava chips and went about her work with purpose. It was a Friday when the wine was ready to sell—three big barrels of it.

Rosa herself did the vending. Her sisters stayed home from school to help her wash drinking bowls. It was many of the guests' first time visiting Zakaria's compound. A good number of them were surprised when they saw his house. It leaned so far over, it was practically on its side.

The wine was strong. Everyone heaped praise on Regina. By noon, people were no longer listening to each other. Even those who hadn't purchased anything to drink were speaking drunken Kiswahili.

It was Stella's first time observing a crowd of drunk people—their words and deeds. Honorata was washing a bowl when Stella interjected, "Honorata! Look! Ah-ah-ah!"

Honorata's eyes nearly fell out of their sockets: someone was taking a piss right next to them. Stella eventually grew accustomed to seeing people peeing on their orange trees, their banana trees, their flowers—even on their house. A zeze player performed in the afternoon. The way people shook their shoulders, you'd think they didn't have any bones in them. The way people stomped their feet, you'd think ants were crawling up their legs. One man had already dug a deep hole with his foot, and he just kept dancing there, digging himself in deeper and deeper—maybe it was to show off his strength. Women danced as well. They stood in front of the men they liked and rolled their shoulders slowly, without moving their feet, tilting their necks to the side. They ululated too. If a man shook his shoulders hard enough in response, the woman took his hand and hoisted it in the air.

While people were dancing to the zeze, a reveler slid up next to Rosa and tried to impress her with his English: "Mai children! We know Anglish Makerere I." Clever, Rosa thought. "Bee-ah. Yes, yes give me my bee-ah." She filled his bowl.

The drinkers sat in little groups. Stella listened as one group ejected one of its members. She repeated the words she heard: "Get out of here, you tick! Buy your own!"

In another group, everyone was laughing. Stella moved closer to listen in. A man was giving a sermon on the dangers of alcohol. Once, he said, someone became so intoxicated that he forgot to cover himself at night with a blanket. Mosquitoes sucked his blood until all that remained was his skin. Another drunkard once slept the whole night in his yard; the following day, he found that his clothes had been eaten by termites. When the man finished with his stories, he asked to refill his bowl.

In another group, two men were arguing about who was richer. "What do you have, you bare-ass?"

"My cheeks may be bare, sure, but I could provide for you and your entire family!"

The elderly were in their own little group. One old man stated that whoever bought him two bucketfuls of booze could marry his daughter. Even though he was not that old yet, Zakaria sat with this group. He bragged that he was an expert at raising daughters.

Regina had given Zakaria a full bucket of wine to drink with his friends. When it was finished, he demanded another one. He threatened to knock over all the wine that remained if they dared cut him off. They gave him his wine.

By six that evening, all three barrels were in the bellies of the drinkers. People swayed from side to side as they walked back to their homes. Others slept there in the yard. When Regina and Rosa added up the day's earnings, they counted two hundred shillings. They were very pleased.

Chapter 4

Rosary, the all-girls school where Rosa was headed, was built along a road hemmed in by mountains. The mountains were dotted with large black boulders and caves that sheltered hyenas. At night, you could hear them cackling, but during the daytime they were nowhere to be found. Five other schools were tucked into the same mountains—all boys' schools. Despite this discrepancy, one girls' school was enough to make the mountains an interesting place to study. From one side, delicate feminine voices could be heard; they were answered from the other side by the sturdy sounds of boys. Only rarely were these voices heard interacting directly—during a discussion or debate, or maybe at a dance. This was the environment Rosa entered: a joyful setting, albeit one in which girls were incredibly scarce. If a girl didn't have a boyfriend, it was no one's fault but her own.

The school was run by nuns, all of them celibate. This seemed appropriate for a school encircled by wild dogs. The girls at Rosary addressed them as "sisters." The headmistress was called Sister John. When Rosa arrived, Sister John was surprised to see her. Many an admissions officer had already begun jockeying to fill Rosa's spot with another student. One officer had told Sister John that they knew Rosa well. "The poor girl," they said. "She drowned while swimming in the lake." Rosa hadn't drowned. She was a month late, however. But she was still permitted to take her spot in the incoming class. Two days after she arrived, Rosa wrote a letter home assuring her parents she was fine and informing them of the difficulties she faced on her journey. She still remembered her mother's words.

Before long, Rosa had made her first friend: her name was Thereza. Every time Rosa visited her in her room, Thereza showed her photos of her male suitors. Rosa couldn't believe how foolish Thereza was. "As for me," she said, "I don't like talking to boys. They never say anything true—I don't even want them to come near me."

She wasn't exaggerating. For the time being, Rosa didn't want to talk to boys at all. When a boy spoke to her, she responded with harsh, dismissive words. Even so, the boarding school boys couldn't bear to see Rosa remain single; she was too beautiful. After one month, Rosa had already received over twenty love letters. She answered all of them with a single line: *Sorry, brother, I'm not able. Try somewhere else.*

Three times a term, school dances were held for the girls and boys from neighboring institutions. Rosa didn't attend even one. On Sundays, the girls were allowed off campus, or to invite friends over to visit. Rosa left school grounds only a few times, and she never hosted anyone. The sisters called her a good girl with a strong work ethic. Sister John was especially fond of Rosa; it wasn't long before she selected Rosa to be class president. Rosa's fellow Standard Nine students liked her as well, all the more because she never competed with them over boys.

Rosa really was a hardworking student; she placed second in her class on the end-of-term exam. That's how she finished her first semester, how she took care of herself. She informed her parents of the day she planned to return home. When she arrived, she found her mother waiting for her with great excitement. Rosa was very happy to see her sisters. While walking around the compound, taking in the changes that had occurred during her semester away, she carried Sperantia on her hip. She didn't see too many changes, actually; the house looked dirtier than she remembered it, and her father had lost some weight. Some, but not a lot.

When people in the village noticed Rosa going to fetch water or to pray, they asked her when she had returned; they kept asking her even after she'd been back for a week. They told her that she'd started to fill out nicely, that she looked fabulous. After a week and a half, everyone was used to her again.

Rosa spent her days reading fiction. You could often find her under a tree, her nose in a book. Other times, she was helping her sisters answer history questions, or helping them do math. One day, Rosa was reading Shaaban Robert's novel *Kusadikika;* her mother was sitting in the shade, weaving a mat; her father was fashioning a hoe handle, using an adze; Sperantia was crying because the doll she had made out of clay had broken, and now she was insisting that Flora reattach its head. This is what they were all doing when Rosa heard visitors calling hodi at the entrance to the compound. Two young men stood before them. One of them had a hat on his head. Rosa didn't recognize either of them.

"Shikamoo mzee!"

Zakaria didn't hear the greeting.

"Mzee, shikamoo!" they said, louder this time.

"And a pleasant morning to you," one of them added.

Zakaria turned to see who the visitors were. "Marahaba. Karibuni," he answered softly, accepting their greetings and inviting them in. He returned to what he was working on.

"Rosa, bring them chairs so they can sit," Regina said.

Rosa brought out two chairs. The young men sat down, facing her. They were still thinking of what to say when Zakaria turned around again and asked them, "So what can I do for you, my children?"

One of them answered: "Sir, we are looking to purchase some eggs."

"Ooh!" Zakaria said. "So all you're looking for is eggs? I have a few I can part with. I can bring them out for you, but the price is ten cents per egg, not five cents."

"Please bring them, sir. Please bring them."

While Zakaria went into the house, the young men remained outside, smiling. Zakaria returned with three eggs in his hand. The young men were inspecting the eggs, squinting at them as they held them up to the sun. Suddenly a whip whizzed through the air and struck their bodies.

"Think I'm an idiot, do you?" Zakaria shouted. "Get out of here, you two!" The young men sprinted away without looking back. They thought Zakaria was chasing them. Zakaria heard them cursing at him once they were at a safe distance.

"You mshenzi! You will rot along with your daughters!"

Zakaria didn't say a thing. Rosa and Regina kept quiet as well. "You're the mshenzi!" Zakaria finally said to Regina. "You bear me only daughters! You bring me nothing but trouble, even here in my own home!" Zakaria fumed.

Regina didn't respond; she was afraid to make fun of him.

Stella picked up the hat and placed it on her head. Her father snatched it away from her.

A short while later, Zakaria calmed down and returned to his work. Rosa's sisters began a game of hide-and-seek. Stella and Honorata hid in little crawl spaces; they hid behind the house; they hid in the kitchen. Sperantia sought them out. After she found them, they went and hid somewhere else. It wasn't long before Stella emerged from her hiding place, crying. Her eyes and nose were swollen. Hornets covered her body. Her sisters laughed and jeered at her, and that marked the end of the game.

The days flew by for Rosa—her leave from school was almost over. One day, while she was bathing Sperantia in a large, curved-bottom frying pan, she heard her mother calling her. Rosa saw the expression of pain on her mother's face. Her father wasn't at home, so Regina told her to go call Bigeyo. Because Bigeyo had her sister over, she said that she would come by later. When Rosa described her mother's affliction, Bigeyo understood; she and her sister ran right over. They found Regina completely incapacitated. They carried her out behind the house, where there was a fenced-in yard; they chased the girls away and told them they needed some space.

Regina gave birth to a baby boy. He was rinsed clean; he cried. Bigeyo ran this way and that, ululating loudly and throwing her hands in the air. Rosa and her sisters came to look at their baby brother. Stella asked why Bigeyo and her sister had tried to kill their mother; she had been spying on them, and had seen them holding Regina's mouth and nose.

Zakaria returned that night. He had already heard the good news on the way home. He picked up the child and congratulated his wife. "Regina!" he said, "Now this compound officially belongs to you!"

"Aksante," Regina answered, smiling. She had the ability, finally, to say something. "Zakaria," she began. "It would help if you put an end to your drunkenness."

"Ah, my wife," he responded right away. "Do you think drunkenness is a disease?" He paused for a moment. "What kind of husband doesn't drink?" he continued. "A nondrinker can never be known the village over. Who here, after all, isn't familiar with Maji Machafu?"

This was his drinking name; it meant "Dirty Water."

"You know, I've been drinking since I was born," Zakaria said. "Booze was my breast milk. If I gave up booze now, it would be like killing myself."

"But Zakaria," Regina responded, "it would help if you at least eased up. Some people drink but are still able to care for their children; and they contribute to work around the house."

Zakaria grumbled, then fell silent, then redirected the conversation. "How much is meat going for in town these days?" he asked. "I'll go tomorrow and pick some up. I'm not sure what else you need."

"Two towels," Rosa answered. "Two sets of kangas and five handkerchiefs. Plus bedsheets. And a mosquito net." Zakaria wrote the items down on a piece of paper so he wouldn't forget. That night, Zakaria sang hallelujah until it was nearly dawn. The next day he went into town. Regina was surprised to see him that evening, returning with all the items Rosa had mentioned.

Regina began to find her voice. She began to express herself with happiness. Even people in the village noted the change. But Zakaria didn't put an end to his drunkenness. He kept on drinking, just as before. And he kept on watching over his daughters as if they were cattle.

For the next two weeks, the women of the village came to give him their congratulations. Each one of them arrived with an offering of flour on her head. The neighbors were happy along with Regina. They wished Zakaria the best, and they hoped that his troubles would subside.

By the day of Rosa's departure, the baby had already been baptized and given the name Emmanuel. He was a healthy child, and his sisters were all very fond of him. Day and night, Stella and Sperantia fought over who got to carry him. As Rosa was about to leave for school, Regina asked if Rosa could have a little spending money. Zakaria gave her an allowance of twenty shillings.

Chapter 5

Back at school, Rosa continued to behave largely the same as she had before. But the new semester wasn't a very good one, for Rosa especially. The novelty of boarding school life had all but worn off for her fellow Standard Nine students. They came back from leave full of cunning and began chatting away in class. And why wouldn't they? The Cambridge exam was a long way off.

The teachers recognized the shift right away. At times, the students talked so loudly that the teachers could hear them all the way from faculty housing. It wasn't just the noise; many students began turning in their exercise books late. The Standard Twelve students had already lodged noise complaints with the head sister. Teachers looked askance at the unruly younger cohort. Every teacher on duty grew accustomed to shushing the students as they entered the classroom.

The students paid no heed. One day, Rosa was summoned by Sister John to her office.

"Rosa," the headmistress began.

"Sista," she answered.

"You must tell me the names of the students who are misbehaving."

Rosa remained silent.

"Rosa," Sister John said again. "If you're afraid to say their names out loud, write them on this piece of paper.

"Sista," Rosa protested, "I don't know who they are!"

"Why not?"

"All I care about," Rosa explained, "is reading books."

"All right then, leave! Toka nje!" Sister John commanded. "Tomorrow, class will be canceled for all Standard Nine students!"

Rosa hurried out of the office. It was better to be punished collectively.

The following day they had no lessons. The entire class was ordered to take up their scythes. Sister John instructed them to cut the grass growing next to the dormitories—all of it. They scythed away until high noon. While they were laboring, the non-troublemakers among them started to grumble: "We shouldn't all have to work because of what just a few of us did. Next time, let's rat them out!"

By the following month, though, the class had calmed down. Rosa wouldn't have gotten into any more trouble if a certain story hadn't found its way to Sister John. It was rumored that three Standard Niners spent the night in the city of Mwanza, and that when they were chauffeured back to school in the morning, they were still drunk. Sister John heard the story two days after the fact from someone who had spotted the girls downtown.

A few days later, Sister John requested that Rosa deliver her classmates' assignments to her office. When she placed the exercise books on the headmistress's desk, Rosa was surprised to hear Sister John ask her to take a seat for a moment.

"Rosa," Sister John began, grinning.

"Sista."

"How are your studies coming along?

"I think they're going well."

"We've been thinking," Sister John confided, "that you would make an excellent nun." Rosa was speechless.

"Rosa, what have you heard over the course of these last few days?"

"I haven't heard anything, Sista."

"Rosa, understand that we trust and believe in you very much. Can you tell me who the girls are who spent the night in the city?"

"Sista, I don't know who they are."

Sister John changed her expression. "Some of the girls are saying that one of them was you."

"Ah!" Rosa exclaimed. "Sista, it wasn't me, it was . . ." Rosa grew quiet.

"If you don't say who it was, you'll be expelled."

"But, Sista, it was . . ." Rosa named the three names.

"Aksante sana, Rosa. You can go now."

Rosa exited the office, sweat pouring from her body.

The three offenders were summoned. The punishment for each of them was to haul one hundred wheelbarrows full of sand. Because they had to haul the sand a great distance, the strongest among them could haul only twenty loads per day. It was a disgraceful, disgusting task; because the campus was close to the road, boys stared at them whenever they passed. Sister John forbade their friends to help them. Their fingers swelled; two of the girls couldn't even pick up their forks at mealtime. After one week they completed their punishment. All that remained was to hunt down the person who had squealed on them.

Rosa thought she would remain anonymous. So she was quite surprised, one afternoon, to find everyone staring at her as she entered the classroom. She opened her desk to take out her textbook and couldn't believe her eyes. She began to cry, audibly. All her exercise books had been torn into little pieces. When she looked over the contents of her desk more closely, she noticed a scrap of paper. She took it out and read: *So that's why you're keeping quiet like this—you thought we'd all be expelled! Whatever happened to your saintliness?*

Rosa went to see Sister John. She explained to her everything that had happened. She didn't yet know that her bedsheets had been incinerated.

The next day the three girls were called into the office again—after Sister John heard that they'd burned Rosa's bedding.

"Which one of you is responsible?" Sister John asked through a muffled laugh.

"Responsible for what?" one of the girls said.

"Did something happen?" another added. "We haven't heard a thing."

"Surely you've heard about the shredded notebooks and torched bedsheets."

The girls said nothing, but they put on a show of looking horrified.

Sister John continued: "It's not such a travesty. Even I used to respond that way when someone slandered me," she said. "If you all were the ones who destroyed her things, it's not so terrible. She's the one who acted like a fool; I didn't ask her to tell me your names. She came and told me on her own."

"That's all we intended," one of the girls volunteered. "To get our revenge."

"So you burned her sheets?"

"Yes!"

"And ripped up her exercise books?"

"Clearly!"

"I knew it was you all the moment I saw this note." Sister John started to pace around the room. When she returned to her desk, she withdrew three envelopes from a book and distributed them to the three girls. Her expression hardened.

"I believe we've had enough of your antics," she said. "And this, I think, is the end of them. You must vacate the school grounds by today at noon. That's more than enough time to pack up your belongings."

The girls wailed. They rolled back and forth on the office floor. "Sista, no!" they pleaded. When they realized crying was no use, they refused to pack up their things. But that afternoon, around three o'clock, police officers came to corral them and take them to the bus station. They were sent back to their respective villages and towns. And that right there was the end of the three girls.

Sister John helped Rosa replace her destroyed items; she helped her buy new exercise books. It was hard work filling in the exercises she'd already done. Thereza helped, and if it hadn't been for her, Rosa wouldn't have finished. The other girls stopped bothering Rosa, but their scorn for her only grew.

They despised Rosa. When she tried to talk to her classmates, they ran away from her and left her all alone. Rosa grew rail thin. It was an enormous struggle for her to finish Standard Nine, but she still managed to place fourth in the end-of-year examination.

When Rosa entered Standard Ten, she stuck to her instincts and kept on fearing and hating boys. When she entered Standard Eleven, Rosa still thought of herself as capable of self-fulfillment.

Her excursions into Mwanza were few and far between. When she went into the city for a change of scenery, she'd take the bus. Rosa stood at the bus stop one day, waiting for the bus to take her back to Rosary; nearby, two boys spoke in blaring voices. Rosa became upset as soon as she heard her name mentioned. The young men hadn't seen her. She ducked behind a nearby commuter and listened carefully.

"I hear that girl doesn't like talking to boys—I mean, like, *at all.*"

"I don't know who she thinks she is."

"I think she's afraid of her daddy."

"Hmm. I've heard he's a real hard-ass."

"The hardest of asses! One day—get this—he lashed us with a whip."

"John was saying that the girl is a kilema."

"Kweli, bwana, it's possible. Even the most beautiful rose has its thorns."

"Kweli, bwana," the other agreed. "But do you really think the girl's made it all the way to Standard Eleven without . . ."

Rosa didn't hear the final words that were said. She watched as the adolescents boarded the bus bound for Bwiru. She could only guess that they were students from the boys' school there.

Rosa remained standing there, silent. The words she'd heard cut her to the core. They disturbed her deeply. She began to think.

Who is this John character? They say that I'm disabled—okay, what is it that's wrong with me? What else could they have meant when they said I'm a 'kilema'? They say my father is strict. What harm is there in that? He's protecting me—isn't he?!

Later that night, as she lay in bed, the words kept swirling in Rosa's head. She made a decision. She made a decision to go out dancing.

Chapter 6

The record is placed on the turntable and the speakers start to shake with sound. Boys jump to their feet and bow before potential dance partners. Young goddesses cross their arms over their chests in displays of refusal. Others— many others—accept. Now is their time to reign as angels. Here, a boy in a suit bows down to a girl and the girl brushes him off; as soon as he turns his back, the girl is whisked off by a boy who's not even wearing a tie. Over there you see another boy; he's asked five girls to dance already and he's not giving up—he's dressed in khakis. It's a wonder, all that's being set in motion inside the club. Young people are dancing. They're dancing to every song. To love songs they're dancing. To songs of death they're dancing. To songs filled with sadness they're dancing as well. There are some people there who aren't students. Others aren't young, but they're dancing with hats on their heads. All the girls have been taken now, they're out on the floor. Off to the side, two boys are in the midst of a debate.

"I'm telling you, Rosa is here tonight. Just a minute ago, she was sitting right here! Where she is now, I couldn't say."

"Rosa really knows how to dance?"

"Wapi!" the boy replies dismissively. "She tries to dance, is all."

"I have to see this for myself!"

The second boy looks out across the dance floor and sees Rosa dancing with someone he doesn't know; he doesn't appear to be a student. The boy sits and waits for the next song.

Rosa trembles in the arms of the man she's dancing with. Her heart throbs against her chest. She wants to tell him to take his hands off her waist, but she can't find the words. "I'd love to know your name," the person holding her says in a low voice.

Rosa wants to speak, but again she struggles to open her mouth. She doesn't have any strength, and she doesn't understand why. She asks herself why her heart is pounding so hard. Slowly, she begins to see that there's a certain something she's been missing. Slowly, she begins to see that she alone can't make herself feel satisfied.

For the rest of the dance, Rosa stays with the same partner. She doesn't want to be passed around among other people. Rosa starts to speak to him.

"You were saying you'd like to know my name?"

"Ndiyo."

"I'd like to know your name first."

"Mine's Deogratias."

"Deo—what?"

"Deogratias."

"I'm Rosa Mistika."

"Asante."

As the dance nears its end, Deogratias leads her outside. As soon as they're out of the club, Deogratias takes her in his arms and kisses her.

"Let me go! Leave me be!"

"Lower your voice," he says to her. Deogratias draws her

body close to his. "I can feel the heat on you. How are you so much hotter than other girls?"

Rosa nearly loses consciousness. She doesn't even know where she is until she hears someone make an announcement: "Rosary girls, all aboard the bus!" When she comes to, she realizes she's fallen to her knees; getting up, Rosa wobbles on her way to the bus. When they arrive back at the school, her classmates have to tell her it's time to get off. "Let's go. We're here." Her thoughts are elsewhere.

Rosa had trouble falling asleep that night after she got in bed. She was too busy thinking. *Will my father find out if I start to befriend boys?* she wondered. *He's back on Ukerewe; I'm here on the mainland. Baba sits there, watching over me—but why? Does he think he's going to marry me himself?*

After a while, sleep carried her away. She saw her father walking down the road with a dog. The dog had a rope fastened around its neck. The dog spotted a goat and bolted after it; the rope snapped, and the dog proceeded to tear the goat into little pieces. Rosa got up. She lay back down, and sleep overtook her again. She saw a young man, thin and with a sizable beard, looking at her with sympathetic eyes. As soon as Rosa saw him, she ran to him, wrapped her arms around him, and cried, "Marry me! If you refuse, my life will be without hope, over!" She began to weep. The boy kissed her and told her, "I'll answer you later on, in a letter; but do you think that after . . ." Rosa woke up again. Now sleep evaded her completely. She got up and slipped on her dress. She went down the corridor to Thereza's room. Thereza was very surprised to see her. It was four-thirty in the morning.

"Can you help me, Thereza?" Rosa said, voice trembling. Thereza had yet to understand what was going on when Rosa leaped toward her and embraced her. They tumbled on top of each other as they fell onto the bed. Rosa started to kiss her but it didn't sate her desire. Rosa needed that scratch-scratch that was one of a kind. The scratch-scratch of a rough beard and a hairy stomach. A fire blazed in the southern regions of Rosa's body. But up north, the fire quickly flamed out.

Rosa's eyes were still bloodshot in the morning. As soon as she finished washing her face, she began searching her room for those letters that had been written to her by male admirers. She couldn't find them all, but those she found she read anew. There was nothing she could do: she no longer knew where the boys were; she no longer knew if they had any interest in her; on top of that, she had already answered all the letters in the same curt fashion: *Sorry, brother, I'm not able. Try somewhere else.* Rosa began to sob. She reached into her purse for a handkerchief to wipe away her tears, and there in her bag she found a short letter. She remembered she'd had the bag with her the night before, at the dance. As for the letter? It was a love letter, asking for her hand in marriage.

Rosa sensed that she had to act fast, while luck was still with her. She thought that the first man to show her affection was indeed the man who would marry her. Rosa accepted. She answered the letter with great tenderness. But after accepting Deogratias's proposal, Rosa entered the arena of romance hungrily, like a dog untethered. She found that one or two boys weren't enough to fulfill her need. That year alone Rosa said yes to five suitors. When Thereza visited her one day, she was amazed to see Rosa had one file full of photos, and another file just for letters.

"You know, Thereza," Rosa explained, "I'm playing around with boys these days like a person driving a donkey. Tug the rope to the right and the donkey turns to the right. Tug it to the left and the donkey turns that way. The donkey doesn't know where it's going, it only knows who's driving it. That's how I'm playing around with boys these days. Not one of these vijana knows where he's headed. Look," she said, "this one here is cross-eyed, but he's still trying to make the moves on me. Just the other day he sent me fifty shillings. Because of his own foolishness—I didn't ask him for it. This one here with glasses is cute, but he was born with six fingers. He's wasting his time. This one here is tall as a tree. I only come up to his waist. Even if he married me, I'd be ashamed to be seen with him. This one is fine as can be, but he has no idea about romance. This one is the jealous type. I don't like men like that one bit."

Finally, she arrived at the photo she loved most. "This one here with the hat on his head is named Deogratias; he goes to the boys' school in Bwiru. He was with us the night of the dance, remember? This is the one who I hope will marry me."

Stunned, Thereza looked on. Her friend, whom she had once considered a fool, had leapfrogged ahead of her. Sensing that her own prowess was now under threat, she spoke up. "Well, if I had wanted to, I could've had forty suitors; I've turned down so many that only two contenders remain," Thereza said, trying to impress her friend. She was also telling the truth; Thereza had learned a great deal about boys. "Some boys I just don't get," she continued. "There's this one boy I totally shot down. I told him that I couldn't like him even if I was forced to. And here's how he responds: 'Thank you so much for your letter: this is clearly a sign you're interested.' It was so annoying!"

"And where did that one come from?" Rosa asked.

"They say—I couldn't even tell you where that giant is from. His legs are as long as an ostrich's!" They laughed together.

"It reminds me of the story of Chameleon," Rosa said after they'd caught their breath. "Do you know that one, Thereza?"

"I don't know it."

"Chameleon proposed to a young girl," Rosa began. "But the girl's father wouldn't allow it. He said to Chameleon, 'Chameleon, begone! You cannot marry my daughter.' Chameleon didn't believe it. He kept looking back as he went on his way—so much that his eyes learned to rotate in every direction."

They broke into laughter again.

"A lot of boys are like chameleons," Thereza said. Her eyes drifted to the handkerchief on Rosa's table. "Who are you embroidering this for?" she asked.

"I'm embroidering it for my boy 'D,'" Rosa answered with pride.

"And have you seen your bestie's boy?" Thereza asked.

"I haven't seen him!"

"He's ancient!" Thereza confided. "You would almost think he's your bestie's father!"

"I wonder why my bestie likes him."

"People say it's because the old man has an automobile."

"Some girls I just don't get!" Rosa exclaimed. "Have you seen the way Mary walks?"

"If you see her walk, you'll be shocked. The way she sticks out her behind—you'd think an airplane was about to land."

"Me, I know someone who wiggles her waist as she walks. She must think it drives the boys crazy!"

Their conversation was brought to an end by the bell summoning them back to class.

By this point, Rosa had already become an object of wonder in the eyes of her peers. She had undergone a radical transformation. In the entrance exam for Standard Twelve, she had placed twentieth in her class. Not only did she fritter away her time sewing and embroidering handkerchiefs, but she began to stay overnight in the city of Mwanza. The sisters were mystified by Rosa's plummeting test scores. But Sister John had found the source of the problem. For some time now, she'd been hearing about Rosa's actions and behavior outside school. One day, Rosa got a ride back to campus—in the car of someone who seemed to be of a certain rank. She was surprised to find Sister John waiting for her. The head sister had received a phone call.

"You'll see me tomorrow morning in my office," she said gravely. The entire night, Rosa lay in bed thinking about what to say to Sister John.

In the morning, when Rosa entered her office, she was shaking with fear. Sister John didn't laugh that day, nor did she feel the need to converse at length.

"Rosa," she began.

"Sista."

"Who dropped you off in their car yesterday?"

"My friend," Rosa said. "My friend who works at the bank."

"Is there another friend you want to tell me about?"

"Yes."

"Who?"

"Deogratias."

"Deogratias! Deogratias!" Sister John repeated. "Rosa, we

have elected to send you home. You'll only return to sit for the Cambridge exam."

Rosa wept. But Sister John had said what she had to say. She was doing her job.

Rosa returned home. When she arrived, she told her parents that she'd been studying too hard at school, and that she'd been instructed to go home and rest her head. Her parents were surprised to see Rosa still resting two months later. It wasn't until her classmates returned to the island on break that Rosa's parents learned the full story. They were very disappointed: they expected Rosa to look after them as they grew older. Regina was the most disappointed.

Zakaria responded to Rosa's behavior by redoubling his efforts to watch over his daughters. Flora now attended a girls' school in Mwanza. When she came home on leave, she was scolded with harsh and insulting words. Honorata was guarded intensely now and was prevented from talking to any boys whatsoever. Emmanuel was cooed at and coddled, cared for best of all. After losing a son between Rosa and Flora, Regina couldn't bear the thought of losing Emmanuel because of her own neglect.

After Rosa was kicked out of school, it didn't take long for her boyfriends to hear the news. They all heard similar stories about her bad reputation. They were told that she'd been spending nights in town, and that she was being brought back to campus by government officials in their automobiles. Many of her suitors, when they heard, searched out her home address and wrote her letters. They sent their sympathies. Rosa noticed that some of them stopped writing her letters after only one month. Slowly, Rosa began losing her boyfriends. Flipping through her file of photos, she became furious and burned all except one—a photo of Deogratias. Deogratias continued writing Rosa letters nearly every week. He praised her beauty repeatedly. Rosa made certain to answer all Deogratias's letters.

One day, Rosa received a lengthy letter from Deogratias. When she read it, she was overjoyed: in spite of everything that had happened, her life was going to get back on track. In the letter, Deogratias assured Rosa that she needn't have any doubts: he was prepared to marry her at any time. He'd enclosed five hundred shillings, to help her while she was home, and informed her that he was ready to sit down with her parents to discuss his proposal. When Rosa finished reading the letter, she kissed it and put it in her file. The room she was sharing with her sisters was now filled with pictures of Deogratias. Two hung from the wall over the head of the bed; one hung over the foot of the bed; and one was under a pillow. Rosa was deeply in love with her fiancé.

While she was home, Rosa had time to study only in the mornings—she spent the afternoons visiting Bigeyo. So when the letter arrived from school, informing her of the start date of the examination, Rosa worried she wouldn't be ready. Still, she was determined to try. When she arrived back at school, Thereza received her with great delight and began telling her about everything she'd missed.

"You know, Rosa, the history teacher realized after it was too late that he was teaching us things we didn't need to know for the test!" Thereza continued to relay tales about each and every subject. She brought Rosa her exercise books so Rosa could pore over them for the three weeks that remained before the test.

When Rosa sat for the history exam, she turned the test

over and over but failed to find a topic she could write about for more than one page. Eventually she settled on four questions and began composing. What she came up with wasn't history, exactly, though it might have been something close. History wasn't the only subject that Rosa found difficult. All of them were difficult except for Kiswahili.

The results of the exam were posted, and Rosa saw that she passed three subjects: Swahili, needlework, and English. The certificate she received indicated that she placed in the third rung of her class. Thereza placed in the second rung. Rosa at least took pleasure in seeing that she had outperformed some of her peers who had been in school the whole year. Thereza was selected to continue on to Standard Thirteen at a girls' school in Jangwani. Rosa was chosen to go to Morogoro Teachers Training College. She was happy. Zakaria and Regina were happy along with her.

Chapter 7

Despite the fact that Zakaria was very strict when it came to raising his daughters, he still wanted to see them married off as quickly as possible. So when he heard that Rosa had found herself a fiancé, he was thrilled. He could already feel the burden being lifted from his shoulders. Around this time, he would often say, "Having so many daughters is a real hassle! You wouldn't believe the number of visitors we get: people stopping by and asking, 'How do you get to so-and-so's?' People who pass through, take a sip of water, then get up to leave." Five daughters in one location did attract a lot of attention. Boys in the area referred to Zakaria's compound as "the zoo."

Zakaria and Regina awaited their houseguest with great anticipation. *But where is he going to sleep?* they wondered. It would be shameful to ask a guest—especially an important one, a guest of honor—to squeeze into an already crowded house. Eventually they decided that he would sleep in the living room. Rosa's sisters all sensed that a special visitor would soon be in their midst—the man who had proposed to Rosa, they heard.

When Deogratias finally arrived, he was given the royal treatment. Each day, a chicken was slaughtered in his honor, and he had ample time to spend with his fiancée. There was only one thing that failed to impress Rosa's parents: Deogratias violated a certain African custom—in truth, he wasn't even familiar with the custom. Deogratias ate with his hat on his head; he didn't even take off his hat when greeting his elders. One evening, while conversing with Zakaria, Deogratias brought up the matter of the dowry he had come to pay. They were seated at the fire.

"Ah, yes, my child, the mahari," Zakaria began. "We've started thinking about it, my wife and I. I can't give you our final answer just yet, but there are some items I can tell you about so you can begin to get your affairs in order. For instance—I don't think you'll be at all surprised to hear this—we need a new house." Zakaria motioned with his head over to their current dwelling. "If you can help me out with the roof," he said, "I can manage the foundation, walls, and finishing. We've also come to the decision that you'll contribute four cows, two goats, a mortar, three chairs, and one thousand shillings. Last but not least, one bucketful of moonshine—for me, personally."

"None of that is a problem," Deogratias responded. "Back home, we pay up to thirty cows for the mahari, sometimes more."

"Don't speak too soon!" Zakaria said right away. "That was only our initial list. I still have to send you to my relatives, and to the relatives from my wife's side of the family, too. You have to ask their permission, as well. After all," he explained, "the child is not mine alone to give away."

"All that is fair as can be," Deogratias agreed. "I'll do it."

The following afternoon, Zakaria offered to show his guest around the island. Deogratias didn't object; it was his first time visiting Ukerewe. The tour consisted of only one stop. Zakaria led Deogratias into a clump of trees that was spitting out puffs of smoke—a fire was burning within and multiple voices could be heard. Deogratias understood. He, too, was a boozer. He could booze it up like a full-grown man. They drank the rest of the day away in the clandestine distillery. By nightfall, people were no longer listening to each other; they talked over one another in loud voices, unguarded, as if in their own homes. Suddenly, Deogratias snapped to attention at the sight of drinkers running every which way out of the clearing. He was still wondering what was going on when he heard the orders being given:

"Arrest them! Freeze!"

The entire thicket was surrounded by police. Deogratias was trapped along with three others, who had taken off their shirts and dropped to the forest floor, so as not to be seen. But as soon as a flashlight shone into the trees, even the smallest ant was visible. Zakaria was nowhere to be found. Deogratias and the others who remained were all apprehended. Their wrists were cuffed close together; if not for the shackles, they would've looked like marimba players. Deogratias began to wail: "I'm a visitor—have mercy on me!"

Two slaps dropped him to the ground. A boot to the chest and another to the stomach finished him off. Blood streamed out of his nose. He cried out in his mother tongue.

"Washenzi!" one of the police officers called the men. "You all are ruining this country for the rest of us. Making us come out in the middle of the night like this. Tonight you savages will be guests of the government!"

Those who were apprehended were forced to march on foot to their destination—a distance of six miles. Because he looked sharp compared to the rest of them, Deogratias was ordered to carry the confiscated moonshine on top of his head.

As soon as they reached the government offices, the men were booked into the compound's jail. It was Deogratias's first time being locked up. They spent two days inside without their case being heard. Deogratias kept spitting on the floor in disbelief. He asked for an audience with the district commissioner, but the guards on duty ignored his request. The dormitory consisted of one tiny room with one window. Deogratias and the others weren't the only ones in the cell. In the corner was a large pail, filled to the brim, the letters *W.C.* written on the side. Across the room was a large blanket, covered in dark spots. The blanket was rough to the touch, like firewood. The first night, Deogratias was wary of getting under it. By the second night, he was the first to crawl beneath the blanket, even though it scratched and scratched at his skin. On the third day, a new arrival recognized Deogratias. He'd seen him before in the city of Mwanza. "What's an official like you doing in here?"

"They caught us red-handed, drinking moonshine," Deogratias explained. "But I was there as someone's guest. I only came to visit my fiancée, you see."

"That's what you're in for? Ha!" the man laughed. "By the time you get out, your fiancée will have already been married by someone else! Me, I stole 20,000 shillings; after I do my time, the money will be right there where I left it. Ha ha ha! 'I was there as someone's guest,'" the man repeated. "Well, I suppose you got what you came for. But wait a second, are you really not married yet?"

"Bado," Deogratias answered. "Not yet."

The other men in the cell laughed until their ribs hurt. Deogratias was finally without his hat. Gray hairs—not a ton of them, but enough—were visible all over his head.

The three days that he spent waiting caused Deogratias to grow thin. By the time he was brought before a judge, he appeared older than he had just a few days before. Rosa and her parents attended the proceedings. Deogratias was well known. He was sentenced to two years in jail. The others he'd been caught with were sentenced to just one.

Rosa learned nothing more about Deogratias until the day she left for Morogoro Teachers Training College. That was when she made the decision to burn all the letters Deogratias had ever written to her, and all his pictures, too. She was on the boat to Mwanza when she heard two women talking.

"That's Rosa. She's the reason Deogratias got locked up."

"You mean Mwanza's Development Officer?"

"The one and the same."

"But he's, like, forty-something."

"And isn't he married to two women already—both of them girls, really!"

"Is it true he got a couple of schoolgirls pregnant?"

"Yeah, but he slipped them some shillings so they wouldn't say it was him. They each blamed a different boy they went to school with."

Rosa heard much more after she arrived in the city of Mwanza. She heard the full story of Deogratias. Deogratias was one of those old men who think of themselves as still young. One of those old men who prefer little girlies—girls young enough to be their daughters, girls who are just beginning to grow breasts. Deogratias was one of those old men who felt no shame. Men who salivated at the small mounds starting to form on a young chest. Men who squandered their time on fleeting luxuries, such as going to dance halls, instead of staying home and looking after their children. Men who tried to blend in among crowds of young people. At the age of forty-two, Deogratias was still writing letters that said, *I love you like a diamond from the mine at Mwadui.* Men like Deogratias were hated by the young. Often, you would hear young men complaining, "These old guys are ruining our chances!" This was the Deogratias to whom Rosa had been engaged: Bwana Maendeleo, Development Officer.

In addition to all that, Deogratias was among those people who used their money and status to get whatever they wanted. Often, you'd see them raised on a stage, exhorting a crowd as if it were the end of days. "Youth of today, you have exhausted us with your recklessness! From this moment forward, anyone seen going out with an underage girl will be locked up! Put behind bars! Anyone who gets a schoolgirl pregnant will be so full of remorse that they'll run out of tears!"

After they step down from the stage, you'll see their Benzes full of underage girls, heading off to a special outing at some unspoiled beach. The girls' parents have nothing to say. What could they possibly say after the big man had already spoken? Slamming your fist against the wall only hurts your own hand. What young person is even going to discuss these girls? A fly doesn't land on the blood of a lion. All over Mwanza, it was well known that Deogratias had run two men out of town because they objected to his advances on their daughters. Excuses were invented to land many a young man in jail.

Deogratias loved dances, especially those schoolgirls' dances. He'd go with his hat. This was how he "encouraged development"—dances, too, are a certain kind of development. This was how he sought out those who gave off heat. At that time, he'd been looking for wife number three, and luck was with him. Never before had Rosa been held in the arms of a man. "Good upbringing" made her love the first man who met her gaze across the dance floor.

Deogratias's two wives had forbidden him to go to Ukerewe to see his fiancée. But after arguing with them and telling them he'd only be gone for a short while, he made a decision to go to the island, despite his wives' protestations that the last thing they needed was an Mkerewe woman in the house. "Wakerewe women love to quarrel," they explained. Deogratias went to Ukerewe and he found what he was looking for.

Rosa stayed in Mwanza for three days. After taking in the story of Deogratias, she intended to cheer herself up a little, to forget the misfortune that had befallen her. She consoled herself with the fact that the world was still full of men. Rosa entered a local hoteli called Green Bar. There she saw many things: the cunning of women and the foolishness of men; women's ability to extract resources and men's willingness to have their resources extracted.

Rosa got a table to herself tucked all the way in the corner. There she sat, enjoying her bottle of Kilimanjaro. Seated nearby were two young men. One was already wasted: his head was flat against the table. The other wasn't quite as drunk. A young woman, a cocktail waitress who worked at the bar, sat perched on his lap; he stroked her waist and groped her breasts. These women were so used to such abuse that it hardly registered. Hovering around them were six other women, also employees of the bar. Bottles littered the table, and not just beer: name-brand liqueurs—Martini, Cinzano—filled the table, as well. After a short while, the young man roused his drinking partner so they could leave. Rosa listened to the young men bid farewell to the females as they made their exit. "Don't try to trick us, you hear? We'll be back tomorrow to pick you up for our dates."

"We belong only to you!" the waitresses responded in unison—their usual line. The two youths swayed their way out the door and headed home to sleep. As soon as the men were gone, Rosa watched the women give each other high fives as they broke into laughter. "Heko! Well done! We really fooled them, no?" she heard. "They spent over two thousand shillings, and tomorrow we'll be nowhere to be found!"

Later that evening, a young man invited himself to Rosa's table. "What are you having, dada?" he asked her.

"Tusker," Rosa answered without delay.

A Tusker brand beer was ordered on her behalf. Rosa drank three bottles. She told the man to pick her up the following day at number 2 Banda Street.

"Just wait till tomorrow, kaka," she assured him. "Then you'll see how delicious I can be."

Rosa was educated by the women at the bar. She knew when she was to depart for Morogoro. She was to depart the following day. Rosa grasped a great deal. She grasped a great, great deal—she understood about love and she understood about exploitation. A woman's love, much of the time, goes hand in hand with a woman's exploitation.

The next day, the young man arrived at number 2 Banda Street. Even his own body had a laugh at his expense.

Part Two

Chapter 8

At the time Rosa matriculated at Morogoro Teachers Training College, it was a school with beautiful buildings and relatively few students. There were even fewer girls than boys, and each student was assigned his or her own room. It was no longer Rosa's aim, when she arrived, to search for a fiancé. She was derailed by just one thing—she loved to please boys. Among the female students, Rosa was the first to gain a reputation. "That girl is mpole and mchangamfu!" you could hear the boys saying—she's polite *and* she's fun! Those who have been drizzled on praise the rain. Each time she emerged from a boy's room, her undergarments showed beneath her dress; she checked her appearance over and over again, self-consciously.

Rosa became known to every boy on campus. She also developed an unusual palate; she began to add a tremendous amount of salt to her vegetables. The girls recognized it before the boys did. It mustn't be, it couldn't possibly be, but of course—she was admitted to the hospital's critical care unit after aborting her pregnancy two months in. Those who were still naive in such matters said to one another, "Who knows, bwana, do you think it's possible she might've been pregnant?" Rosa stayed in the hospital for two weeks. The boys all prayed for her rapid recovery.

Rosa recovered. She resumed her dance. But during the weeks that followed, she worried herself thin. Boys gossiped about her in little groups; Rosa could see that she was the subject of their conversations. She began trying to ambush them, to find out what exactly they were saying. It wasn't long before Rosa spied some boys looking over a newspaper together. She hid nearby and listened to their words.

"I haven't tried that particular style yet."

"Why don't you go to the maabara, bwana, and give it a shot?"

"Remind me again where the maabara is?"

Rosa listened until the end of the conversation. She was able to infer that they had assigned her the name "maabara," or "laboratory"—a place for conducting experiments. If you mix this chemical with that, you get such and such a result; if you add more of this chemical, you get a different result. Rosa was called "Lab" for short. She didn't care; the name didn't bother her in the slightest. *Kama Mola hapendi ni kazi bure, watasema watachoka,* she'd sing along to the song on the radio. If the Lord doesn't will it, it isn't any use. Let them speak until their throats are sore.

In Morogoro, Rosa didn't receive many letters in stamped envelopes. If she got a letter with a stamp and a postmark, she assumed it came from Thereza. One day, Rosa received a stamped letter that took her by surprise. Written on the envelope were the words *For Roza.* She opened it right away. The handwriting on the letter inside was barely legible. It was as if it had been written by someone who attended adult education classes, the kind that met under a tree.

Namagondo
P. O. Box—
NANSIO (Bukerebe)

To my daughter Rosa,

*I hurd you were in the hosbital and gave birth to a baby boy.
I Regina along with my drunkard of a husband am greatful
to God. We ourselfs werent blessd with many boys. You have
birthd a boy and we are very happy about it. We have already
thought of a name for him. You'll call him Bagaile. This
wouldve been his uncle. He drownd when his canoe tippd over
on the way to Mwanza. Little Emanuel is doing well, hes not
nearly as light as he was befour.*

Its me,
Your Mother Regina

Rosa folded it up and tossed it in the wastebasket.

Her mother, who had in fact just taken an adult literacy
class that met under a tree, put a great deal of effort into
writing Rosa the letter. She spent a very long time composing it, after being told by someone from Dar es Salaam that
Rosa had given birth. The intermediary had passed through
Morogoro by bus on their way to Ukerewe. Because the bus
paused in Morogoro only briefly, they hadn't been able to
hear the full report. One week later, Rosa received another
letter, from her sister Flora. Flora extended her condolences. While attending "Jela" (the nickname of the girls'
school she went to in Mwanza, which was guarded by police), Flora had also gotten an abortion. *A pregnancy alone*

can't make me drop out of school and ruin my life, Flora ended her letter.

The life of a human is like a tree. A tree needs water, air, and light. If a tree is denied ample light by the trees around it, it grows taller. It tries to surpass the trees nearby, so it can get to the light. Zakaria denied his daughters light when they needed it most. He hit them; he prohibited them from talking to boys. Like trees, they reached toward the light and grew and grew in height until they could no longer be cautioned by anyone. With daughters, you'll often find that the mother builds them up and the father knocks them down; with sons, the father builds and the mother knocks down. All this results from a lack of understanding regarding the mother's sphere of influence versus the father's. The world is changing, however; we are the ones changing it. Let us agree, finally, that the days of locking our daughters inside and anointing them with oil are over. Ours is not a world to be told about, as in "The world is like this and like that." Ours is a world to go out into, as in *see, decide, act.*

Rosa had another abortion at the beginning of her second year at the teachers' college. Some said it was her third time getting pregnant; others said it was her fourth.

Rosa was now well-known throughout Morogoro, even in the city center. Eventually, news of her reputation reached the city's clergy. A priest was dispatched to the college to remind Rosa of the light of salvation. Upon his arrival, the priest asked for the location of Rosa's room. He heard a young man shout from his window, "What's he looking for? Lab? Well, what are you waiting for, bwana? Take him over there!" The priest didn't understand; he was led to Rosa's room. Rosa was studying her exercise book when she heard the call at her door. She opened the door and the priest entered, Bible in hand. Rosa shut the door behind him.

"I'm sorry for wasting your time," the priest began, placing his hand on his chest. He glanced at the table. Rosa's exercise book was wide open. "Oh, I see!" he said approvingly. "You were studying."

The priest picked up the exercise book and looked over its contents; he began by skimming its subject headings. There in the book, he came across strange things. Rosa had written a great deal about people: *Short women . . . Tall women . . . Types of . . . How to know that a boy likes you . . . How to conceive a boy versus a girl . . . Positions good for . . .* All the subject headings were elaborated on in great detail. Finally, the priest came to the page Rosa had been studying when he entered the room. The priest read the page:

Question: Can taking birth-control pills decrease a woman's desire? Yes, it can. It's common for many women to experience a drop in sexual desire. But the upside of these pills is that the fear women face—fear of an unwanted pregnancy—is eliminated completely. Bodily desire stems from emotional desire; desire is more than simply being in heat. When a woman is on the pill, her heart will be calm, without fear. In fact, for many engaged or married couples, the pill brings about a peace of mind that actually increases bodily pleasure. People can use other birth-control methods, but their lovemaking will be impacted. The pill will have no such negative side effects. There's no reason for an intelligent person to believe that taking birth-control pills interferes with the world's natural order more than unwanted pregnancies—unwanted pregnancy after unwanted pregnancy.

The priest stopped reading there. He reread the final sentence three times and shook his head with sorrow. Rosa had underlined the words that were most important to her—the subjects that troubled her the most and the topics she needed to explore more deeply: *bodily desire; fear of an unwanted pregnancy; eliminated completely; bodily pleasure; methods; unwanted pregnancy after unwanted pregnancy.*

If the priest had spoken to Rosa about any of these matters, maybe he could have helped her. But instead, he began to speak of salvation. Shortly after he opened his mouth, Rosa realized that he wasn't just wasting her time—he was wasting his own.

"Rosa, those words you wrote—where did you get them?" he asked, humbly.

"I got them from my peers," Rosa answered.

"I am begging you: burn them." The priest paused for a moment. Then he spoke again: "Rosa, I have come to assist you; I have come to lead you back to the light of salvation."

"You've come to assist me?" Rosa said in disbelief. "Am I a charity case?"

"Yes," the priest answered. "Your soul is impoverished."

"How do you know? Are you God?"

"An evildoer is known by their actions."

"And how have you come to know about my actions?"

"Smoke follows fire," the priest replied. "Have you never gotten pregnant, not even once?"

"Gotten pregnant by whom?"

"That I don't need to know."

"You'll see if I get pregnant again."

"I am God's servant," the priest stated. "I have brought you the good news, Rosa."

The priest opened his Bible to a page he had bookmarked with a picture of a man on the cross. Rosa attempted to listen as the priest began to read.

"John 8: 1–10. 'And they went, every man unto his own house; and Jesus went unto the Mount of Olives. And in the morning, when it dawned, he entered again into the Temple, and all the people came unto him; and he sat down, and he was teaching them. And the scribes and Pharisees brought unto him a woman discovered in the act of adultery; and they sat her down in their midst. And they said unto him . . .'" The priest read until the end. And then he read the final words again: "'And Jesus said unto her, *Nor do I pass judgment on you. Go on your way and sin no more.*'"

The priest closed his Bible. He began to sermonize: "Don't despair, Rosa, don't despair. Despair is an unforgivable sin. Jesus is still with you. In this passage, we see him forgiving the sin of the adulteress. Salvation still shines in your eyes."

Rosa vomited the priest's words back at him; she couldn't hold them down any longer. "What does 'salvation' mean anyway? Salvation? What salvation!" Rosa declared. "If there's a hell, so be it! I'm headed there!"

"Don't be so enraged, Rosa," the priest cautioned.

"Hapana," she said. "You have no idea what hardships have befallen me."

"Everyone on earth experiences hardships," the priest replied.

"Father, my life is already ruined, and I don't care!" Rosa said. "Why should you care more about my soul than I do myself?"

The priest looked at her, amazed. He stood and opened

the door. Before stepping outside, he exclaimed, "Lucifah! Lucifah has taken possession of your soul!" The priest exited the school with haste, his Bible tucked in his armpit. Rosa closed the door. That was the last she saw of the priest.

Rosa had stopped caring what people thought about her. She knew herself, and that was all that mattered. From that point forward, she did the very things that people accused her of, right in front of the accusers. Each boy who paid Rosa a visit yawned with satisfaction as he emerged from her room. It was a scandal.

Rosa acted this way because she was angry. "Sijali!" she would say. *I don't care!*

Another reason she acted this way? The birth control pills she had already purchased.

Chapter 9

The rain was falling and Rosa sat hunched over in her room, a kanga wrapped around her shoulders. She sat tranquilly, waiting for her hour to arrive. Rosa had been invited out. Usually, on days when it rained, students didn't enjoy themselves much; their freedom of movement was restricted. Rosa alone was happy that day.

The cold was severe. And all the students were shuttered in their rooms. Outside, hardly a creature could be seen. Not a single bird was visible in the sky. The only exceptions were the prisoners being marched back to the jail at Kinguruwila; corrections officers walked behind them, rifles in hand. The inmates carried bundles of firewood on their heads; each bore his own burden. Their clothes were drenched, and the rain was still coming down. On the road, an overturned fuel truck, wheels in the air. The driver had been rushed to a hospital in town; if not for the prisoners, the driver would have died at the scene.

The rain stopped around noon. After eating, students went and gawked at the overturned vehicle; the school wasn't far from the road. Students were allowed off campus on Saturdays. A good number of those who went to look at the vehicle continued on into town. Rosa had other matters to attend to—more pressing affairs.

After her meal, Rosa returned to her room and sat on her bed. She looked at her wristwatch. It was still early: her watch said it was one o'clock. Her heart beat forcefully against her chest. She picked up the exercise book that she'd been told to burn and turned to the page the priest had read. All of a sudden, Rosa remembered how she'd responded to the priest that day. *Mapadri watu wa ajabu! You men of the cloth are a bunch of freaks!* She realized she had spoken the words out loud; she got up and peeked outside to make sure no one had heard. She sat back down on the bed, buried her head in her hands, and started to think. She startled herself with a series of yawns that went: "Haauu . . . maisha . . . isha . . . isha!" She stood and stretched her arms over her head as she continued yawning. She looked at her watch. The hour was approaching. She read the letter again and confirmed when she'd been told to arrive. The letter said four o'clock; her watch now said two o'clock. She began to prepare herself.

Butone brand bath soap was sought out. When she reached the bathing stall, she began to admire and caress herself. She used a full hour to wash and rinse. When she finished bathing, she opened her trunk and considered what to wear. Black wouldn't do: she'd look like she was in mourning. White was too easily soiled. She dumped all her clothes out of the trunk, sat on the bed, and pondered her choices. Finally, she decided on a white dress with vertical black stripes. She tried it on and found that it fit. A mirror appeared—*come and see the one you admire.* Rosa began to smile as she looked at herself. She parted her lips and examined her teeth; they were clean. She stuck out her tongue; it was clean and healthy looking. She opened her mouth wide and looked inside:

everything looked good except her hair; it was all tangled. Rosa looked like someone else, someone other than herself. A woman doesn't overlook oiling her hair, just like a man doesn't neglect taking a razor to his chin. Hair oil was applied. Now it was time to select which shoes to wear.

A pair of high heels slipped onto her feet. She took a few steps in them, struggling at first. As she walked the length of the room, gracefulness came into her strides. Rosa looked at her watch and saw that it was five o'clock. She inspected herself in the mirror a final time. She spotted some powder on her ears and wiped it thoroughly with a handkerchief. She grabbed her handbag and exited the room in a hurry. She locked her door.

Rosa wasn't going far. She had been invited over by a certain teacher from her very institution—the College Chancellor. When Rosa arrived, she found the Chancellor anxiously awaiting her.

"Karibu! Karibu!" he welcomed her. "I thought you weren't going to make it!"

"Ahadi ni deni," Rosa replied. A promise is an obligation.

"Asante."

Rosa sat down on one of the sofas. Before she said anything else, he asked, "Which do you prefer, Martini or VAT 69?"

"Martini," Rosa replied, fanning herself with a handkerchief.

A bottle of Martini brand vermouth was brought out. Rosa started to drink. She studied all four sides of the living room. One wall was filled with newspaper photographs. On another wall hung an assortment of diplomas and certificates. On a third wall hung a huge portrait of the Chancellor and his wife on their wedding day. On the fourth side of the room was a display of sculptures, carved in the distinctive style of the Wamakonde. Rosa took it all in. The side of the room she found most attractive was the one with newspaper photos.

"Rosa," the Chancellor began, after finishing his first goblet of wine. "Rosa," he said again. "You're well aware that the other instructors hate you, are you not? Just the other day we had a faculty meeting. The instructors all agreed that you should be expelled from school—yes—because you had an abortion. But as this institution's lead educator, I can assure you that you won't be expelled."

"For that, I'll be forever thankful," Rosa said, batting her eyelashes.

"I'll also see to it that you're awarded your teaching certificate."

"Asante."

When half the bottle remained, the radio was turned on and the dance of seduction began. The curtains were pulled. By the time the bottle was empty, Rosa was sitting with her thighs exposed.

The sun set. Darkness entered. A huge moon appeared. When the Chancellor emerged from the bedroom—at eleven o'clock—and went outside to shut a door that had been left ajar, he was surprised to see the moon staring down at him. The moon was scarlet, as if to pass judgment on him. He closed the door and hurried back inside.

There in the bedroom, the head of the institution—Thomas—asked Rosa to undress so they could lie down; it was getting late. She requested that he look away while she removed her clothes. He obliged, turning his back to her. Thomas could see Rosa's shadow on the wall, slowly stripping. Now he was in trouble. His heart thumped against his chest. Rosa had on nothing but a towel.

"Where can I find some sandals? I want to bathe first."

"Under the bed."

"I see them. Bafu wapi?" Rosa asked.

Thomas spun around. He showed her to the bathing stall. Rosa followed behind him.

"Hii hapa." *This door here.*

When she finished bathing, she found Thomas waiting for her in the bedroom. Rosa was wearing a single kanga. Thomas watched her every move. Very slowly, she dried her body with a towel, then combed out her hair. Thomas was losing precious time. He stood up and took hold of Rosa; he pressed his body against hers and kissed her. They sat down on the bed. They stood up again. They kissed one another and pushed each other onto the bed, kissing passionately. Thomas spread his palm across Rosa's breasts like a person holding two eggs in one hand. They sat on the bed again, hearts throbbing. They kissed, over and over again. Thomas touched Rosa's chin with one hand while the other hand caressed her waist. Slowly, he tilted her face toward his so they locked eyes.

"Rosa, we can't go on like this all night," Thomas said. "Let's turn off the light and go to bed."

"Ngoja kidogo," Rosa said. *Wait just a little.*

She applied a few drops of oil to her skin. After a short while, the light was extinguished. It was pitch black now. Rosa sat down and Thomas heard the mattress squeak. Finally, she was in bed with him. Thomas reached for her with an enormous craving. Rosa was completely naked. He pulled her toward him.

Immediately, his arm was shoved away.

"I don't normally do this," Rosa said.

"Why not?"

"I just don't want to. This is our first time being together, is it not?"

"Come on!"

"Let's just talk."

"For how long?"

"For as long as I wish."

"And how long will that be?"

"Try to be patient."

"That's not possible," Thomas said. "Why can't you?"

"I just can't," Rosa tried to explain.

"But why don't you want to?"

"My circumstances don't allow it."

"What circumstances?"

"I'm your student."

"Forget that."

Thomas reached for Rosa again. Rosa sent his arm back.

"Fine," Thomas relented. "I'll go sleep in the other room."

Thomas sat up. He hadn't left the bed yet when Rosa grabbed him and brought him back. Rosa embraced Thomas. Thomas was enveloped, pulled in.

The moment Thomas felt Rosa's body, he no longer knew where he was. He was done for. He uttered many a word. He swore up and down that Rosa would never be expelled from school. Rosa had won. She wiped the sweat from the brow of the College Chancellor: after nation building, the good citizen perspires. That night, Thomas was like a chick beneath a hen's wing. He was so gathered in that he didn't hear another sound. Even if someone had been walking on the roof, Thomas wouldn't have noticed.

The birds began to sing. It was only dawn, but a voice was still audible inside the house: *Kiss me slowly; you are hurting me, dear!* Outside, a suitcase was by the door; someone listened at the window. They became enraged when they heard the cry of pleasure issue from within. They'd heard enough; they departed for a neighbor's house.

When the individual who'd been listening at the window returned, they were like a person gone mad. They began tearing down the door with an axe. Siku za mwizi ni arobaini: sooner or later, even a skilled thief's luck runs out. The couple inside the house was astonished to hear the door being dismantled with such fury.

The College Chancellor realized that this was his wife; he had been caught in the act before. Rosa sobered up instantly; she darted this way and that, like a fish in an aquarium. Now the door to the bedroom was being torn open; it burst into pieces. His wife entered with her axe raised, ready to bring it down on Rosa's head. The Chancellor snatched it away before it fell.

"Leo utanitambua!" she said. "From this day forward, you will recognize me! You want to bring your whorish ways upon me, is that it?"

Rosa tried to run, but the woman grabbed her and knocked her to the ground. The woman bent over her; her teeth sank into Rosa. Blood spurted across Rosa's face. The woman appeared to spit something on the ground. Rosa screamed. The Chancellor pulled his wife off Rosa, and Rosa ran. Before she even made it outside, a radio struck her in the back. It fell to the floor and shattered into pieces. *That Rosa!* Into the bedroom went the two who remained.

Alone in their bedroom, the College Chancellor was scolded like a little child. "You thought I went back home, didn't you?! I am about to explode! I am tired of this msi-chana! If you are going to marry the girl, you had better do it quick!" She picked up the axe again and began smashing a cabinet, followed by a pair of bedside tables. "I don't know why the State bestowed any importance on you," she said. "You only got this position because of tribalism. Me, I know it. And now I can finally expose you. If it weren't for this lit-tle job of yours, you never would've been able to marry me! You're as black as a cooking pot!"

The Chancellor, Thomas, was someone who understood marriage to be a life shared by two people, husband and wife, until they had their fill of each other—not until death! This woman, now on her way out, was his third wife. Thomas had used trickery to get rid of his wife without having to tell her he wanted her gone. The day he wrote the letter to Rosa, he left it on the table, in plain sight, when he went to teach—just after his wife had informed him when she was going to visit her parents.

When Rosa arrived back at the school, she entered her room as quickly as she could. Even so, there were some girls who saw her. As soon as she reached her room, she locked herself inside and rushed to find a mirror. When she looked at her reflection, she couldn't believe it was her own face staring back at her. Rosa burst into tears. She wept for her ear. The woman had clamped down on it and torn off the en-tire outer lobe. Rosa felt very sharp pain, now that the shock had subsided. At nine o'clock that morning, the Chancel-lor came and drove her to the hospital—right after finding a chunk of ear in his house.

The wound healed. But now Rosa had just one good ear. Even after she recovered, she kept her head wrap on.

Students often asked themselves why Rosa hadn't been expelled yet. Her actions were known to the entire faculty. Following this latest deed, news of which spread that very day all the way to Dar es Salaam, Rosa was known as the wife of the Chancellor. It was an open secret that it would be very hard for her to be kicked out of school. The students began to resent her; anyone the Chancellor spotted talking to her was given a harsh punishment. One day, when she passed by a group of boys, one of them spat on the ground. "That one there has no more use," she heard. "She's all used up!"

Rosa looked back at them. The young men fell silent. She opened her mouth but, because of her anger, words refused to come out. She had better just bear it, she figured; she continued on her way to her room. Rosa didn't realize what was going on until she passed a group of girls and heard one of them say, "Maskini! Poor thing, she doesn't even realize!"

Rosa turned her head to look at her behind. She saw that her clothes had ridden up, wedged themselves into her buttocks. The young men had been disgusted when they saw her; that's why one of them had spat. When Rosa got to her room, she threw herself onto the bed. A great many matters swirled around in her head.

Rosa, she heard a voice calling to her from within. It sounded like the voice of someone who was about to die. It was the faintest of voices. Rosa alone was able to hear it. Rosa alone was able to recognize it.

Rosa, Rosa, Rosa, my child. I am dying. Come close so I can feel you; come so I can give you my final blessing.

It was the voice of her mother, and it troubled Rosa deeply. Since being in Morogoro, Rosa hadn't managed to go home during any of her breaks from school. On one leave, she went to Dar es Salaam; on another, she went to Moshi; on her most recent leave, she was in Tanga. Back then, at the time of her trips, Rosa was still very well-liked by boys; now young men spat when they saw her. Back then, her fellow females tipped their hats to her; they admired how she conducted her own affairs. Now they pitied her to the point of calling her "maskini." Back then, she had two ears; now she had one ear. Life was swindling her, again and again.

She remembered her mother. She remembered her mother's words, too. She remembered her siblings: Flora, Honorata, Stella, Sperantia, and Emmanuel. She remembered how Stella made them all laugh, and the stories they told each other at night. Tears welled in Rosa's eyes. She wiped her face with a handkerchief. She felt even greater sorrow when she recalled that she had received three letters from her mother, informing her of her sickness. Her mother had been ill. Regina had asked her to come home during leave. Back then, Rosa didn't think too much about the letters. Now she felt anguish. Rosa made her decision.

She resolved to go home on her next leave. When she arrived, she found her mother in decent health. Rosa had already worried herself thin, but her mother was okay. She'd had Rosa on her mind. Regina received her daughter with open arms.

"Mtoto wangu!" Regina welcomed her. "Come sit upon my knees!" Rosa didn't refuse; she sat upon her mother's knees. The two of them shed tears as they embraced. "Rosa, how have you grown so thin?" her mother asked. "What have you been eating?"

Rosa didn't answer. When she hopped down, her mother went and fixed her something to eat.

When Rosa's sisters came home from school that afternoon, they were elated to see her; Rosa was happy, too. Stella spoke up first.

"I'm in Standard Six now," she announced. "Honorata didn't pass. She just hangs around the house these days while the rest of us go to school."

"Has Flora come home yet for a visit?" Rosa asked.

"Ndiyo," Stella answered. "She was here with us on her last leave."

"I hear that she's lighter than I am these days."

"Mmmh! Says who? When it comes to skin tone, you two are about the same."

"Where has Honorata gone off to?" Rosa wondered.

"She said she was going to get her hair braided," Stella remembered. "Maybe that's where she is."

"What schoolyear is Sperantia in?"

"Standard Three. She placed second in her most recent exam."

While Stella was being interviewed, Sperantia arrived home and went to change clothes. Stella went and did the same. Regina brought them what was left of the food she had offered to Rosa. Rosa listened to Stella talking with her mouth full. "That's Honorata coming now," she said. Honorata returned from getting her hair braided at her friend's place. She greeted Rosa and began asking her about Morogoro: what the people and the land were like. Rosa described the Waluguru people: what they looked like, the clothes they wore, the foods they ate, the work they did to sustain themselves. She described Morogoro's mountains.

Zakaria didn't arrive home until later that night, as was the norm for him. Regina informed him that Rosa was inside. Zakaria just grumbled and said, "Who is Rosa, again? I've never had a whore as a houseguest, let alone as a daughter."

He spoke the words in a loud voice. Rosa heard them, and they troubled her deeply. She didn't care if she heard such words spoken by other people. But by her father? This was a grave, most serious matter. At that moment, Rosa was like a prodigal child returning home. She needed to be received with open arms and instructed gently. At that moment, Rosa needed people to calm her. Just the notion that there were people who cared about her was enough to settle her heart and bring about a measure of happiness. Among the major mistakes made by her father, this was the second worst.

Rosa cried. She began to question whether Zakaria was really her father. She wondered whether she was his legitimate child. But Rosa wasn't a child anymore. She was an adult. She wiped her tears away with a handkerchief and said to herself, *Ya Mungu mengi. God is vast,* she acknowledged. *God is the one who knows who has erred. If I hadn't been born here, maybe I would've been another person.* Rosa made a decision. For now, she would keep quiet. Her insides churned like she was about to vomit. But for the time being, no one knew how she felt.

While Rosa was home, her mother showered her with care. Every day she was given ample milk to drink, more than any of her siblings. After two weeks, Rosa began to gain back some weight. Everyone at home felt great sympathy for her except her father. When she gave her account of how she lost her ear, they all listened with hands pressed against their cheeks. No one laughed at her. But Rosa didn't share the whole story. She described how she'd been mistreated by the woman without having done anything wrong.

It wasn't long before Rosa quarreled with her father. During her visit, she happened to get acquainted with the District Commissioner, in no small part because he was Thereza's older brother. One day the D.C. came to pick up Rosa in his car to go to Rubya Beach, where the sand is as white as sugar. When he pulled up in his vehicle, Zakaria was lying down. He woke to the rumble of an engine; Rosa was already dressed for her excursion. Zakaria gave the District Commissioner an earful as soon as he stepped outside.

"Go on home with your fancy car! You think that there are so many girls here that you need a vehicle to transport them? Toka hapa! Get on out of here with your ears as big as a donkey's! And you, Rosa," he said, "don't even peek your nose outside! Don't let me see you walking out that door! Do you think you're in Morogoro?"

Rosa had already decided what she was going to say. She had just been waiting for the right opportunity. Now Zakaria had poked the beehive. Rosa rushed outside and strode up to her father. She spewed out the words she had nurtured in private for a long time.

"Each and every moment you watch over us. Do you think you're going to marry us yourself?" Rosa finally spoke the words, the words she'd needed to say since that day she was beaten, back when she was a girl. Zakaria heard her loud and clear: the words he'd needed to be told that day. The words pierced Zakaria's heart. Stunned, he stood in silence. Her shoulders high, Rosa swaggered back and forth, victorious. Before her stood a behemoth of a man she had defeated without spilling a drop of blood. The behemoth's blood had frozen inside its body, and the District Commissioner was there to witness it.

To preserve his honor, Zakaria parted his lips. The following words came out of his mouth: "Rosa, from this day forward you are no longer my daughter."

"From this day forward," Rosa shot back, "you are no longer my father." Right after she said it, she climbed into the waiting vehicle and proceeded to that special beach. Rosa didn't come home that night.

Later in the evening, Ndalo dropped in to visit his neighbor. He found Zakaria sitting in his living room. After they finished greeting each other, Zakaria shook his head and said, "Ndalo, the world has gotten off course."

"What do you mean?" Ndalo asked.

"Today, today, my daughter defied me. She renounced me. She said that from this day forward, I am no longer her father!"

"Sema kweli!" said Ndalo in disbelief.

"I'm telling the truth!" Zakaria insisted. "Not only that, she said it in front of the District Commissioner. Right to my face."

"Sema kweli!" Ndalo said again.

"Ah!" Zakaria replied. "You think it's a lie?"

"The truth is," Ndalo admitted, "I'm a bit surprised myself. But you aren't the first person to be treated in such a manner. Just the other day, a certain mzee was told something similar by his daughter. Why? Because he didn't allow her to wear those new garments that make women look like jigger fleas. I don't know what they're called . . . eh, I forget the name. They're called something like 'teti' . . . 'tahiti' . . . 'taiti,' that's it, 'taiti,'" he said. Skintight skirts.

"All the children who go off to school are the same," Ndalo continued. "I heard about another mzee, over in Bulamba. He stabbed himself in the tongue because his children forced him to eat with a fork. Maybe we'd be better off not sending our children to school."

They conversed this way for a long while. It was like two blind people trying to show each other the way. They couldn't see the other side of the situation, and who was losing out. They didn't consider that a lot of young people were just as frustrated with their elders.

"Today's old people are always bringing us down," the young people would say. "When they come to visit, they refuse to use toilets. They insist on hanging their asses out over the bush." On only one matter do the elderly and the young agree: that the world has gotten off course. Back in the day, a nickel could buy you an article of clothing; these days, it doesn't even get you a kitumbua. Back in the day, it was forbidden for a woman to consume poultry; these days the mister, the missus, and the children all sit down at the same table. Compromise occurs when one group takes a step forward and the other group takes a step back.

Rosa waited for her father's anger to subside. After two days, she returned home. Fortunately, she didn't find her father there. She found her mother along with her sisters. Stella described how Zakaria had sharpened his panga and threatened to cut Rosa into little pieces if she came back that first night. Rosa's mother advised her to pack up her things and leave quickly, before Zakaria returned. She told her to go to her godmother's. Rosa didn't object. She packed her things and went to her godmother's in Kameya, around five miles away from Namagondo.

Chapter 10

All told, Rosa stayed in Kameya about two weeks. When her leave from school was nearly through, the District Commissioner arrived in his automobile and escorted her to the port in Nansio. Rosa boarded the ferry. As the boat turned its back to Ukerewe, Rosa pivoted to take in the island. People were waving farewell. Rosa put her hand up, too, but privately she was thinking about her sisters and her mother. She trusted she'd see Ukerewe Island again before too long: she was on her way to finish her final semester. She already saw herself as a teacher.

Aboard the ship, Rosa happened to sit near a woman with a baby in her lap and became lost in thought. The baby was very handsome, enough to make Rosa feel envious. He looked at Rosa and grabbed at the band of her wristwatch. He smiled at her and reached out his little hands. She wanted to pick him up.

"Mtoto, njoo," she called to him.

The baby lifted his arms in the air. His mother let him go to her. She was more than happy for some relief. In Rosa's arms, the baby showed no sign of wanting to cry. He began feeling his way around Rosa's chest. Rosa knew what he was looking for. She dangled her watchband in front of him to distract him, and he began to play with it. The entire time,

Rosa was wondering if she, too, would give birth to a beautiful baby like this one someday. She started to feel pangs of regret as she recalled the pregnancies she'd aborted. But Rosa wasn't old: she was still young and she was still fertile. This was her consolation. For the moment, at least, her mother's words had no power.

While these thoughts circled around in Rosa's head, the baby became sleepy. He drifted off, perched on Rosa's lap, face upturned and mouth open. Rosa got to work shooing away the flies so they wouldn't land on his lips and find their way into his mouth. She felt no fatigue. She felt the baby's heart beating quickly. She felt the baby's rapid breaths. All this Rosa observed with wonder. Rosa looked at the baby. She gazed at his still-shut eyelids. Rosa wasn't seeing a baby before her but rather a little angel.

"Some women have the magic touch," the child's mother started to say. "He usually isn't much of a people person, but today you picked him up, and he fell fast asleep in your arms. Dada"—sister, the woman addressed Rosa—"my child really loves you."

"Maybe he was already tired," Rosa responded, smiling at the compliment.

When the ferry arrived in Mwanza that evening, Rosa was surprised: how had it crossed the channel so quickly? But the ship hadn't been going any faster than usual; the crossing had taken three hours, just as it normally did. Rosa was sorry to have to part ways with the child. Her arms had been warm, but as the boat docked the warmth dissipated, and a chill entered her body. Rosa remembered that she had a packet of cookies on her. She gave them to the baby and bid him farewell.

Rosa didn't go out that night in Mwanza. The following

day was a Sunday, the day schoolgirls were allowed to have visitors, and Rosa wanted to go and see her sister Flora. When she arrived at the turnoff to Flora's school, around one o'clock, she was surprised to find it cordoned off and guarded by police.

"Shida!" Rosa said under her breath.

"Njoo hapa!" Come here! a police officer called to Rosa. Rosa obeyed. "Who are you here to see?"

"Dada yangu." My sister, Rosa said.

"You're too early. You have to wait until two."

Rosa waited in the sun for a full hour. The entire time she was thought to herself, *This is exactly what I hate: being watched over like livestock. They think this is really the solution. They think this is really the way to prevent schoolgirls from getting pregnant! These people don't understand.*

"What's your name?" the police officer asked her.

"Rosa."

"Rosa who?"

"Rosa Mistika."

"Mistika is your father, then?"

"No, Zakaria."

"Who are you here to see?"

"Dada yangu," Rosa said again.

"Your sister doesn't have a name?"

"Flora."

The police officer wrote it down.

"Haya! You can go in," he informed her. "But you must go see the teacher on duty before you visit anyone."

Rosa began walking toward the school. Barbed wire surrounded the entire campus. She assumed the school was nearby—it wasn't. The checkpoint had been set up far away, to create a buffer zone. Finally, Rosa saw some buildings.

When Rosa arrived at the school, she saw an mzungu, a white woman, seated in a chair. It was her turn on duty that day. Some other people—young people—were standing there pleading their cases.

Flora spotted her sister and ran and stood next to her. She wasn't able to take her inside or even greet her without permission from the teacher on duty.

"Who are you here to see?" the teacher asked Rosa.

"Flora."

"What's your relation to her?"

"She's my sister."

"What's your name?"

"Rosa."

"Which year is your sister in?"

"Standard Twelve."

The nun opened the notebook in which Standard Twelve students wrote their guest requests. "Her name isn't in here."

"Sista, this is my sister," Flora said, speaking up for Rosa.

"If you forgot to write her name down, too bad. You can't see her."

"Sista!"

"The rules are the rules. And we must follow the rules."

"Sista," Flora pleaded.

Flora held firm in her pursuit of permission to speak with her sister. Eventually, the nun took pity on her. Rosa was allowed in. Flora took her sister off to the side. They hadn't been given permission to go very far, so they spoke in Kerewe to limit how much they would be understood. Flora was the first to speak.

"Rosa, this school is so strange. We are guarded like little children. They think that even while we're on leave, they need to watch over us. But a lot of girls have already gotten pregnant right here at school, and they've been expelled," she explained.

"That's your problem. The Rosary schoolgirls don't have it nearly as bad. Flora, you know how baba and I have fought because of matters like this?" Rosa said. "This issue of being guarded like little children? Well, he renounced me, and I renounced him. What did he ever contribute to my education anyway? Not a single banknote."

"I heard all about it from a certain boy," Flora said. "I already forgot his name, though."

"Flora," Rosa said, "let's see some pictures of your wa-vulana!"

"Let's get out of here."

Flora took Rosa to her room and brought out a large file of photographs. She gave it to her sister. Flora stood behind her and began to guide her through its contents.

"This one here I'm no longer friends with. He says I should pay him back for all the money he spent on me, but he's not getting a thing. I never asked him to treat me. This one I like, but he hasn't bought me a single bottle of soda. This one's from a very poor area. This one here I'm getting really friendly with. He's crazy light-skinned, and he's thick. You know, Rosa, I don't like a man who's skinny. He's from the south, this one. He's nice and plump—a real plunderer. His name is John. My heart belongs to John; only John can marry me. You know what else I don't like?" said Flora. "A young man who doesn't know how to dance. After tying the knot, you'd just sit at home, like a plant in a field waiting for rain. But John really knows how to dance. You know what else? Anyone who wants to propose to me is going to have to go to the hospital and get tested, and I have to be there to see it. Some men will try to fool you. One guy already infected me with some things," she volunteered. "But I've made sure that John is disease-free."

"Flora," Rosa said. "I'm getting married soon. If baba doesn't allow it, I'll marry myself off."

"You've already found a new fiancé?"

"Yes," said Rosa. "Our College Chancellor."

"Pole sana." Flora offered her condolences.

They sat quietly for a while. Rosa wasn't sure what Flora's condolences were for. "Emmanuel was well when you last saw him?" Flora started up the conversation again.

"I didn't stop by the compound when I was leaving," Rosa explained, "but I'm sure he's fine."

They sat in silence again.

"Who gave you permission to bring your guest in here?" a nun suddenly erupted at them. She booted them both outside and instructed Rosa to leave immediately. Rosa said good-bye to her sister and climbed aboard a bus headed back to the city. There on the bus, she overheard a young man speaking to his friend.

"Shule hii! Hii hapa!" This school here, he indicated. "They're free for the taking, albeit guarded. They even get picked up by the cooks at the Indian restaurants in town. Because they're always guarded," he went on, "they've become like animals. They fall for anyone that happens to cross paths with them. They've lost their ability to choose."

Rosa listened closely. She almost voiced her agreement, but she stopped herself; her voice wouldn't be heard, she reasoned.

Eventually, she reached the hoteli where she'd booked a room. She intended to scope out the scene in Mwanza that night, but after she finished eating her dinner, she figured she had better take a nap first. She stretched out on the bed, figuring she'd get up soon. An image of the little baby she'd held on the boat came to her and then sleep carried her away. When she awoke, it was midnight. Rosa decided to go back to sleep.

The next day, Rosa boarded a bus bound for Morogoro. As soon as she got to the school, before she even went to her room to put away her things, she went to see the Chancellor. Upon arriving at his house, she found only children there.

"May I see the Chancellor?" Rosa asked.

"He's bathing," one of the children answered.

Rosa sat down on one of the couches; she was surprised to see that the Chancellor had purchased multiple new couches, a new table, two large standing cabinets, and many other items. More than the furniture, though, she was surprised to see the two children. When the Chancellor finished bathing, he came to see his guest. Rosa stood.

"I'm sorry, maybe I'm mistaken. I'm looking for the Chancellor. Has he moved out?"

"You're looking at him," the man said. "Is there something I can help you with?"

"No, it's not you. Bwana Thomas?" Rosa attempted.

"You're looking for Bwana Thomas?"

"Ndiyo," Rosa confirmed.

"Are you a student?"

"Ndiyo," Rosa said again.

"What's your name?"

"Rosa Mistika."

"All that is just your first name?"

"Ndiyo."

"I can speak to you in my study."

"What for?"

"Bwana Thomas gave me a message to give to you."

"A message for me?"

"Ndiyo."

"'Ndiyo,' as in he's no longer here at the school?"

"I'll explain," the man said.

Rosa waited for the explanation. "Shall I give you the message inside?" the man suggested.

"I think that would be best."

"Come in and take a seat," he said. "I'll be right back."

Rosa took a seat in the study. She thought that the man was a visiting instructor, perhaps. "I'm Bwana Albert," he introduced himself when he returned. "I've been brought here to take the place of Bwana Thomas. I'm asking you to sit like a student and converse with me using proper manners. Do you understand?"

Rosa began to tremble.

"I'm sorry to tell you that Bwana Thomas has been removed from his position. He's in Tabora now, with his wife."

Tears trickled down Rosa's cheeks. She took out her handkerchief and wiped them away.

"Rosa, did you receive my letter?" Bwana Albert asked. As Bwana Albert spoke, Rosa sobbed louder and louder.

Albert showed Rosa out and shut the door. Tears streaming down her face, she found her way to her room. Fortunately, no one saw her; most of the students hadn't returned yet. When she arrived, she collapsed into the chair next to her desk. She put her arms on the desk and buried her head in them, crushed. In her heart, she'd already determined to let Thomas marry her. She was thinking about Thomas when she heard someone call hodi at the door. Slowly, she got up to open it.

"Samahani, Rosa." Excuse me, said the girl at the door. "I have a letter for you from the head of school." The girl handed her the letter and went on her way. She seemed to know, somehow, the words it contained. Rosa shut the door. She opened the letter very slowly. The letter was typed. She took it in.

Rosa lay down on the bed. The tears that poured out of her were enough to fill a teacup. Her head pounded. While Rosa was in her room, she thought about how God was persecuting her. Outside, Bwana Albert was addressing the students, describing what his new administration would be like. From inside her room, Rosa could hear the applause. She wondered if the students were cheering her expulsion. After the meeting, she heard students saying, "Lab sasa itafungwa!" as they walked by her room. Now the Lab will be closed for good! Other young men spat as they passed. Rosa heard them; she grew even more upset.

It was as if the world outside had disappeared. Rosa searched her room for a rope but came up short. She took the belt off one of her dresses, but it wouldn't do. Eventually, she remembered she had a pocketknife in her clothing chest. She rushed to open the chest, so she could put an end to her misery before her anger subsided. Rosa found the knife and unlatched it. She cut open the front of her dress and prepared to insert the blade. As she felt the tip of the knife touch her stomach, Rosa closed her eyes. She slowly began pushing it into her abdomen. Her outer layer of skin had already been punctured when someone gripped her hand. Rosa startled; she was in the arms of Albert.

"Don't do it, Rosa!" he urged as he restrained her. "You cannot profit from such foolishness."

After his assembly with the students, Bwana Albert had come to tell Rosa to pack up her trunk; she was being expelled, permanently. In some way, he felt sympathy for her, but he had to follow the rules. Rosa was taken and locked in a small room—after making sure there was nothing inside she could use to harm herself.

That evening, Rosa was brought food. She was like a prisoner. There in her cell, Rosa reflected on many things. She thought about what she would tell her mother. She thought of what she would say to her sisters. Eventually, she thought about what trickery to employ to avoid being sent home. It wouldn't be easy: the new chancellor seemed like someone who didn't like kidding around. The entire time she'd been at his house, he'd shown no sign of laughter or amusement. Rosa worried that her life was falling apart at the worst possible moment. She was like a runner at the head of a race who tripped one step from the finish line.

Bwana Albert was still young. After he got his teaching degree from Makerere, he was sent right away to be the chancellor at the teachers' training college in Mpwapwa. He was known to be strict, and for his hardness of heart. He had yet to marry, but he was caring for two of his brother's children. *No girl dares to giggle in his vicinity,* you'd hear the boys at Mpwapwa say admiringly. This qualification of his— if it can be called a qualification—earned him a reputation. Eventually even the government recognized him as someone capable of running a school. And Albert did perform the job well: when he was at Mpwapwa, the students adored him; nary a schoolgirl became pregnant on his watch. When

Bwana Albert began his post at Morogoro, he continued to lead by inspiring fear.

First thing the next morning, Albert took his car and drove Rosa and her belongings into town. After Bwana Albert made sure that she had boarded her bus, and that the bus had departed, he returned to campus. Rosa felt bitterness and anguish at having been expelled from school.

Bwana Albert had removed the main stem of the conflict. He was pleased to have done so without causing a major disturbance. That entire day, students speculated about what had happened to Rosa: some said she was dimwitted; some said she was a lunatic; some said she'd had a poor upbringing; and so on and so forth. But many others praised her, saying no other girl conducted her life quite like Rosa did. Whatever the case, Rosa had been expelled.

Bwana Albert didn't speak of Rosa again. That evening he headed home, thinking about what he could do to repair the school's reputation. As soon as he arrived, he shut himself in his room so the children wouldn't come climbing on his back and make him lose his train of thought.

Darkness entered. To the east, signs of rain, or a storm gathering. After a short while, heavy black clouds covered the entire Morogoro area. The darkness was profound. When Albert opened a window to look outside, a flash of electricity blinded him, and he slammed the window shut. Rain pounded against the roof. It was a true tempest—even those with corrugated metal roofs feared that they'd be ripped off by the wind. Everyone expected to hear, the following day, that so-and-so's house had blown away or fallen over. Every time a bolt of lightning struck, people thought it struck just three or four yards away. People curled up in their beds. Sinners confessed their misdeeds. Those who weren't wicked themselves theorized that thieves must have brought about the storm.

Albert didn't entertain thoughts such as these. He was serious, hardworking; the storm didn't frighten him. After he closed the windows, he returned to the task of sorting class schedules. Like a boy holding on to a special promise, Albert felt no fatigue. He kept on working while he cooked his dinner. He used an electric burner. Albert was drawing a series of rows when he saw something snakelike slither across the floor toward the fridge. It disappeared underneath it. Just then the lights went out. Albert understood. He thanked God that the snake hadn't touched his foot. He went to light a kerosene lamp. After he lit it, he went and took two sodas and a loaf of bread from the cupboard and began to drink them with the bread.

Bwana Albert had finished one bottle of soda, and half the loaf of bread remained when he heard a knocking on the door. He listened. He had heard quite a bit about wachawi—wizards—recently. He listened closely. He didn't hear another sound. He said to himself, *Maybe it's just the wind.* He heard a knocking on the door again, more forceful this time. Albert got up very slowly. He got out his panga—the only weapon in the house—and approached the door. Secretly, he was still scared. Machete in hand, he pressed himself flat against the wall, ready to chop at whatever was about to emerge. No one opened the door. He waited. He heard the knocking again. This time he heard a voice saying, "Mwalimu, hodi." Teacher, can I come in? Immediately, he thought of his students. *Maybe some calamity has befallen them over at the school,* he said to himself. *Maybe someone was struck by lightning.* "Wait!" he said, finally, in English. He put away his panga.

Albert cracked open the door very, very slowly: he was still somewhat afraid. As soon as it was open wide enough, someone slipped in. The figure before him looked wretchedly poor, and ancient, dressed in a head covering that obscured their face. Their soaked clothes clung to their skin, and they shivered from the cold.

"Wewe nani?" Albert asked. The figure was silent.

"Wewe nani?" he repeated. "Don't you understand Kiswahili?"

No answer. Only silence.

"Wewe mchawi?" Are you a wizard? Albert inquired.

Albert tried to remove the person's head covering so he could see their face. The person refused to be uncovered. Albert heard them crying. Then, the person began to remove their head covering and reveal their face on their own. They were starting to become recognizable. They were poised to speak. Albert had a terrible urge to hear what they were going to say. So when they opened their mouth—very, very slowly—Albert showed every sign of listening intently. Finally, they began to speak.

"Albert! Albert!" Tears flowed from their eyes. They continued: "Albert! Albert! What did I ever do to you?"

Albert was silent, dumbfounded.

"Albert! Albert!" they cried out. "This is impossible!"

Albert held them, hugged them; he no longer cared that his clothes were wet. The woman's tears trickled down onto Albert's arms. He tilted her face up, and their eyes met.

"Rosa. I cannot help you."

Rosa sobbed and heaved. Albert took mercy on her. His

heart had never before been struck with such pity. He nearly began shedding tears himself. He got ahold of himself. It's not customary for a man to shed tears, he reminded himself.

"Rosa, how on earth have you managed to return?"

"I turned back midway," Rosa explained. "I got off the bus somewhere near Dodoma, and caught another bus back to Morogoro. I figured that if I went home," she added, "baba and mama would be very disappointed."

Albert drove her in his car back to her old room. The following morning, he called an all-faculty meeting. He described to the instructors the condition Rosa was in. He described to them how she'd almost killed herself with a knife. Albert told the faculty members that it wouldn't be difficult to let Rosa return: he hadn't yet informed the Ministry of Education of her expulsion. The teachers didn't argue. They agreed. They took pity on Rosa. But she must desist from her old behavior, they said.

Rosa was permitted to finish the school year, and she studied as if her life depended on it. She was determined to show those who despised her that her mind was sane, her intellect sound. Two weeks later, final exams began. Rosa came perilously close to failing, but she passed, and was satisfied with her relative triumph. She had indicated, in her list of preferred posts, that she'd like to teach in Mwanza Region. Indeed, it was her first choice. Rosa didn't want to be far from the district she came from anymore; she didn't want to be far from her mother.

When the placements were announced, Rosa learned she'd been assigned to a primary school in Nyakabungo, Mwanza. There, she hoped to embark on a new existence.

Chapter 11

If you ask someone out in the country what their life is like, they'll tell you: "Life in the country is good, brother. The cool air keeps the head clear. Without all the racket, a person can think. There's no dust. Everywhere you look, there's greenery, and trees with beautiful, sweet-smelling blossoms. Inhale the gorgeous scents: first, they tickle your nose before winding their way to the back of your throat. In the country, my brother, you see how everything grows: the beginnings and ends of things. When water is scarce, you hear people crying, 'This year, there's going to be njaa!' Famine. You hear people invoking God, because so much in the country depends on rain. A country dweller lives alongside livestock and understands the relationship between humans and animals. If you see someone milking a cow, you'll probably also see a little child squatting off to the side, waiting for their portion of milk. If a cow or goat dies, a country person mourns the loss, sheds tears. And cow manure makes excellent kindling once it dries, my brother. Lo! It makes the whole compound smell better than incense. Some cow piss here, some nanny goat piss there—and over there some big strong billy goat piss. The entire compound smells wonderful; no rosewater can compete! Let me tell you, my brother:

in the country, you'll hear birds singing from the early dawn all throughout the morning. What music can surpass that?"

"I only eat my vegetables cooked in ghee!" you might hear a country person say. "When a country person goes out for a walk, their dog is there to greet them when they return home. See the hound wagging its tail, barking, and baying. When a country person sits and eats, their dog stretches out beside them, close but not begging. On the other side, you might see a cat stretched out in the same way. After the person is finished eating, the dog and cat chew on the bones. A child who grows up in the country is taught never to let anything distract them from their food; if they glance away, the next thing you'll see is a chicken escaping with a piece of fish in its mouth, with a child in hot pursuit. The child despairs, then goes to their mother, looking for sympathy. But the child gets a scolding instead. From a young age, a child of the country is taught to live around different kinds of creatures. Not just animals, but birds, too. My brother, country people are children of the sun, moon, stars, and rain. What child raised in the country doesn't remember running around in a downpour, naked as the day they were born? Country dwellers look up at the heavens to determine when to plant which crops. What child raised in the country hasn't been filled with pride at being the first to see the moon emerge? Out in the country, there's no shortage of entertainment. No one spends money to watch a dance competition or a sporting event!"

Rosa was a child of the country, but notions such as these were no longer in her head. When she selected Nyaka-bungo Primary School as her top choice, Rosa wasn't thinking about life in the country. The school was right there in the middle of urban Mwanza.

When Rosa received her teaching certificate, she was overjoyed. It also made her think back on how she had pulled one over on Bwana Albert. Now that she had the certificate in hand, she no longer needed to ingratiate herself to any teacher. So when the bus pulled out from Morogoro, bound for Mwanza, Rosa was looking forward to changing the direction of her life. She didn't want to be called a malaya—a whore—ever again. She'd done her share of carrying on. Now it was time to give it a rest. Romantic matters didn't excite Rosa like they used to. If someone called her "Darling," it no longer gave her butterflies; it was just an ordinary word. *When I arrive in Nyakabungo,* Rosa thought, *no man is going to set foot inside my home. No man is going to play around with me.* These were her thoughts now. These were her expectations. But the school at Nyakabungo was right in the city. Where was Rosa going to see animals in their natural habitat? Where was she going to find plants? Where was she going to breathe that clean, refreshing air that would clear away the cobwebs in her mind? More than that: Where would she hear the morning birdsong that contains life's secret?

With hopes of setting her life on a new course, Rosa made her way to Nyakabungo. She thought that she would find faculty housing there; she was taken aback when the school principal told her that she would have to look for a room to rent in town. Rooms were incredibly scarce in the city of Mwanza, and the few that were available were very expensive. After three days of searching, Rosa found a room in a house on Lumumba Street. She didn't stay there very long; the reason she gave for leaving? Within the walls of the house were women who thought everything was for sale, even communicable diseases. The knocks at her door were so frequent that Rosa had to vacate. "I can't even prepare my lessons," she'd complain.

Rosa moved to Uhuru Street. She found a nice room and took good care of herself. Many people knocked on her door at night, but she never opened it, not even once. Before long, young people started to curse and despise her. "Una-ringa nini wewe!" they began to say. *Just who do you think you are!* Rosa didn't care. She didn't let their words get under her skin.

Not only did young men hate Rosa; young women hated her, too. And it's more dangerous to be hated by a woman than by a man. At that moment, Rosa didn't know who her enemies were. It didn't occur to her that there were people who detested her. She continued to take good care of herself.

Rosa did her job as a schoolteacher well, too. When she got out of class at four-thirty each afternoon, she would go straight home. She would bathe, then return to her room. In her room, she would read and knit. After a month, her room was very nicely decorated.

One day, while she was bathing, a woman went into Rosa's room. Rosa didn't see her, but some of the other women at the house on Uhuru Street did. The woman entered Rosa's room, then left in a great hurry. All in all, she wasn't even in there for two minutes. As the woman left, she told Rosa's housemates who were seated outside, "If Rosa asks about her pen, tell her that I'm the one who took it. I'll give it back to her tomorrow at school."

"Who are you?" the women asked.

"A fellow teacher at Nyakabungo."

"Please stay," they tried to persuade her. "She's just bathing, she'll be done soon."

"Thanks, but I'm in a hurry," the woman said.

Rosa heard none of this from inside the bathing stall. By the time she finished, the woman was already long gone.

"You had a visitor," her housemates informed her as soon as she emerged. "They said not to look for your missing pen. They'll give it back to you tomorrow at school."

"What was their name?" Rosa asked.

"They didn't say. All they said is that they're a teacher at Nyakabungo."

"A man?" Rosa assumed.

"Hapana," the women corrected her. "A girl."

Rosa couldn't figure out who the visitor was. At Nyakabungo, there were no teachers who were "girls." Her female coworkers were all middle-aged. Upon entering her room, she found that her pen had indeed been taken. The pen had been engraved, with her name on it; Bwana Albert had given it to her. Rosa trusted she'd get her gift back the following morning.

When night fell, Rosa began preparing her evening meal. She transferred water from the storage jar into a metal pot, to boil for her ugali. As soon as the water began to bubble, Rosa was surprised to see that it had changed colors. It was blue. She thought that maybe she had boiled something by accident. Rosa poured the water out and started over. Before adding water to the pot, she carefully inspected the contents of the storage jar. The water in the crock was clean and clear, as it normally was. When she boiled it, it changed colors again. Rosa dumped the water out just in front of her door. She washed the pot and drew fresh water from the tap. She boiled it and saw that it was fine this time. She prepared her ugali, ate her meal, and was satiated.

The following morning, Rosa was still in bed when she heard people yelling, alarmed. "They wouldn't have survived this! They wouldn't have recovered! They would've died on the spot. Maybe someone did die. Call the police! Call the police!" Rosa got up to see what was going on. When she tried to open her door, she was surprised to find that the door had been blocked by an enormous termite mound. Rosa climbed out through her window—and that's when the people in the street reported to her that what she had nearly drunk was an extremely powerful poison. If she had ingested it, she would have died immediately, without emitting so much as a cough. Many people in Mwanza had already died as a result of this poison. Those who were lucky enough to dump or toss it out found that large mounds had sprouted up the following day, wherever they had poured the liquid. When she heard the news, Rosa began to tremble. For the time being, she had no way of knowing who had tried to poison her. She did expect to find out who had taken her pen.

Rosa refused to go to the police before doing some investigating on her own. At school, she asked her female colleagues if any of them had come to visit her the previous evening. They all denied knowing where her room was. When she asked about her pen, they denied any knowledge of that as well. Although she kept up her investigation, Rosa remained in the dark for a long time about who her archenemy was.

Then one day, Rosa passed by a bar in the city center. She saw a girl standing in the doorway; the girl was staring right at her. Rosa kept walking, but she didn't get very far before she heard her name mentioned. She pretended not to hear.

"I hate that teacher so much, I can't even tell you."

"Where is she?" Another woman came outside to sneak a glance at her.

"That savage there—that's the mshenzi who ruined my life!" the first woman said. "I don't know how she managed to survive. She should be in her grave right now."

"What did she do?"

"She's the one who got us expelled from school back at Rosary! She snitched on us! If she hadn't ratted us out, I wouldn't be here in a hoteli, working as a barmaid."

Rosa was too far away to make out anything further, but she turned back to look at the girl's face. The girl ducked into a nearby house. Rosa was afraid to go and confront her; she didn't want to trouble herself, so she went home. When she got there, she asked her housemates and neighbors about the woman she'd seen. Rosa was told by those in the know that, long ago, the woman had attended Rosary, the girls' school. Rosa was told the woman's name and which street she lived on. Later on, Rosa crossed paths with her at the market. She looked at her closely: she knew her. The woman really was one of the girls who'd been expelled. Rosa couldn't interrogate her right then. There were too many people around.

When the woman left the marketplace, Rosa followed her. Rosa was the first of the two to speak. "Samahani dada." Pardon me, sister, she began. "I think I've seen you before someplace, but I don't remember where."

"You forgot about us as soon as you became a teacher, Rosa. Asante!" the woman said. Thanks for nothing!

"I remember your face," Rosa replied, "but I've forgotten your name."

"You destroyed my life. I pray to the Lord to make your life as miserable as mine."

"And that's why you tried to poison me to death?" Rosa shot back. "Fortunately, God doesn't abandon his creations—I'm still alive."

"Don't slander me just because your lovers want you dead!" the woman said. Rosa became incensed. She grabbed the woman and tried to shove her down, but throwing a barmaid around wasn't so easy. A crowd of onlookers grabbed the women and separated them before they knocked each other to the ground.

"Let them fight!" a young man yelled. "When women fight, they're bound to rip off each other's clothes—let's have a look! Free entertainment!"

Some people laughed. But others in the crowd ignored his words. Rosa was ushered away from the fracas, and the woman went the other way, toward her home.

In the days that followed, Rosa was hypervigilant: she was afraid of getting poisoned. She persisted in taking good care of herself. She didn't invite anyone into her room. Young men began to fear her; their propositions fell on deaf ears.

Rosa's reputation spread throughout the city. Eventually, the news reached an instructor who taught at Kirumba Primary School, there in town. He was also new to teaching, in the middle of his first year. For a long time, though, he'd been looking for a girl to marry. All the girls he'd been with previously he rejected out of hand, because they still went out with other men. He was looking for a woman with a good reputation—like Rosa. After he heard talk of her chastity, he began asking where he might find her. Eventually, he learned the location of her rented room—its number and its street address.

Rosa was ironing her clothes when she heard someone call hodi at her door. Because it was still afternoon, around four-thirty, she opened the door. As soon as she opened the door, a young man, thin and with a sizable beard, walked in. It was like Rosa was dreaming. She looked into the young man's eyes; they were full of sympathy. She could see her future. *This kijana is not like the others,* Rosa said to herself. *I think he comes bearing good news. God willing, let him say the word.* Rosa didn't know who the young man was, but in his eyes she saw a promise: the husband she had seen in her dream.

"Karibu kiti." Have a seat, Rosa offered graciously.

"Thank you," the man responded, "but I'm in a hurry."

"Then you're welcome to say your piece."

"Thank you," the man said again. "I have just a short message."

He pulled out a letter and gave it to Rosa. Rosa received it. The young man said good-bye and went on his way. When Rosa opened the letter, she looked down and saw the name of its author right away. She read the name *Charles Lusato.* Rosa had long forgotten where she'd seen the name before. After thinking, she faintly recalled having seen that name in another letter. Rosa had received so many letters that she didn't remember who Charles Lusato was. For a time there, Rosa had had quite a few boyfriends; she didn't recall this Charles.

The letter itself was a love letter. Charles hadn't disguised his intentions. He stated clearly that he was seeking a woman to marry. *Rosa, I feel that it's you,* Charles wrote. He went on: *I've seen you many times in town, from afar; but I've just now summoned the courage to compose a letter.*

Rosa saw she had better try her luck one last time. Being proposed to was a serious matter, she now saw, one that occurs only rarely. *This kijana must marry me,* she resolved privately. *If I turn him down, that's it, my life will be over; I won't have anything to hope for, ever again.* Rosa let loose her final arrow. *If the arrow goes astray, that's it,* she concluded. *The giant—life—will have slayed me.*

The whole night Rosa thought about the young man. All of a sudden, she remembered she had once gone to school with someone named Charles, back when she'd been in Standard Seven. The harder she thought, the more fragments she gathered. Eventually, she recalled the whole story. She remembered how she'd walk to school with him; she remembered the letter; she remembered how she was beaten by her father; she remembered how she'd been dragged over to Ndalo's house that night. She saw her father throwing Charles's five measly shillings back at him. The more the memories flickered to life, the more her love for him increased. He was her husband, the one whom God had scripted into her life from the beginning.

When Charles returned the following evening, Rosa had already made her decision. Rosa looked at Charles closely as he entered the room: yes, he was the same Charles, but now he had a beard. She welcomed him in. After Charles took a seat, Rosa told him she was unable to answer him in spoken words. She placed the letter she had written on the table but told him not to read it right away. "You can read it later," Rosa said, "when you're by yourself at home."

Charles went on conversing without knowing what the contents of the letter were. He felt like a fool. *I can't go on talking without knowing whether the answer is affirmative or negative,* he said to himself. He asked for permission to go relieve himself, and Rosa showed him to the bathroom.

Charles opened the envelope while he was in the stall. Inside, he found a single piece of paper. His hands were trembling. On the full-sized sheet of paper, he found only a few words.

Mpenzi Charles,

Thank you very much for your letter. Take me. Embrace me. I am yours forever. I give you my heart; I give you my breath, my life. I am yours in every way. Here I am, holding out my hand. Take this hand, mpenzi, and lead me through this valley of tears.

She who loves you always,
Rosa

Charles was satisfied. He was pleased. He received the answer he was expecting. He returned to Rosa's room with a smile on his face. After he sat down, Rosa began to speak. "Charles, do you remember me?"

"To be honest, I'd forgotten you," Charles admitted. "But yesterday, as soon as I saw you up close, I remembered you."

Rosa looked Charles in the eye. His eyes radiated love. Charles understood. He moved toward her, took her in his arms, and kissed her. They remained like this for a long time. Finally, they let go of each other and sat down.

"Rosa," Charles said. "Rosa, do you remember that day?"

"Siku gani?"

"The day our love was severed when it was still tender and new?"

"I remember," Rosa said. "But grass regrows after a cow

grazes. Fire scorches a field, and the field comes back lusher than before."

"So you agree with your father," Charles ventured. "You think people who set fields on fire aren't interfering with the natural order of things?"

"Charles, what my father did hurt me more than you can imagine. Oh, Charles," Rosa sighed, "if parents could only understand that a single action of theirs can destroy their children's lives, they'd grasp the weight of their authority and be more careful."

"Rosa," Charles said, steering the conversation in a new direction. "Where have you been since the time we parted?"

Rosa recounted her tales from Rosary and Morogoro Teachers Training College. Charles recounted to Rosa his tales of Mkwawa and the teachers' college in Marangu. They didn't say good-bye until it was midnight.

This was how Rosa became reacquainted with her friend from long ago. This was how Rosa became engaged to be married again. She finally felt that her life had returned to normal. And Rosa really did love Charles. The following day, she was the one who went to visit him.

Charles was a fine host. After Rosa finished drinking the tea he made for her, she turned her attention to some articles of clothing she saw hanging on the wall. "Which way to the laundry room?" she asked.

Charles snatched the clothes away from her. "You're a distinguished guest," he said politely.

Rosa embarked once again on a life of romance—and Charles also loved Rosa. He took her out to go dancing, to the cinema, and on excursions outside the city, to take in the fresh air. Eventually, people had to admit that the engagement was genuine, not something they had announced rashly. Those who took pleasure in spoiling engagements were forced to give up; they might as well try to pluck salt from seawater.

Rosa paid Charles many additional visits. In the privacy of Charles's home, they would often kiss. One day, Charles tossed Rosa onto the bed; he couldn't take it any longer. Rosa clenched her eyes shut: she, too, was in a terrible state. Charles closed the windows and doors. Rosa stretched out on the bed, cooing like a dove. Charles began to kiss her again; they moved each other this way and that. Very, very slowly, Charles lifted up Rosa's dress. Rosa felt Charles's hand on her. His fingers were continuing to explore when an idea suddenly entered Rosa's head. She grabbed Charles's hand and moved it gently away from her body.

"Charles, not today," she said.

"When, then?"

"On our wedding day. It's better if we wait until the day itself."

"That's impossible."

"Just endure it a little while longer. I'm begging you, don't ruin me before it's time. Charles . . . I'm a virgin."

Rosa struggled to utter those last words, faltering as she said them. As soon as Charles heard the words, he went numb. His desire to stroke and caress Rosa vanished on the spot.

"You are the one I've been searching for all this time," Charles told her. "Rosa, I have the utmost respect for you."

They let go of each other. Rosa had said the word, that word that's harder to say than all others in today's modern world. And Charles believed it: he recalled the day when

Rosa had been beaten by her father; he remembered how careful Rosa had been not to speak to him again. Charles loved Rosa more and more, especially now, because of this. From that day forward, he revered his fiancée. He was afraid even to kiss her. He waited for the day of the wedding.

Rosa and Charles's engagement became widely known. Kijana after kijana began to speak of it as if it were their own, as is their custom. Eventually, one kijana volunteered to talk to Charles. He went and picked him up from his house and took him to a local hoteli. The kijana was also a teacher. Rosa hadn't seen him around town; Charles had gotten to know him as a drinking companion. They went to a quiet bar where they could converse in private. After a couple of beers each, the kijana—the young person—started in: "Charles," he began, "I heard you found yourself a fiancée."

"Who told you?"

"It's just something we're hearing," said the kijana. "We don't know if it's true or not."

"Whoever told you has tricked you," Charles said.

"Charles, if you're keeping a secret from me," the kijana warned, "then I'm not going to tell you the words I came here to convey. I have a very important matter to discuss."

"What kind of matter?"

"It's about your fiancée."

"But who told you?"

"Forget it. Let's just finish our drinks and be on our way."

"You can't leave before telling me your story."

"Tell me your story first."

Charles began to divulge: how his life first intersected with the girl's, back when they were just kids; how they separated; how they found one another again in the city of

Mwanza. When he finished his story, the kijana ordered two more bottles of beer.

"I feel sorry for you," the kijana began. "This woman is not marriage material. If you trust me, you should leave her right away, starting tomorrow. Rosa—isn't that her name?" Charles nodded. "How do you think I know who she is? She took care of me—pleasured me. When we were in Morogoro, she was passed around like nobody's business!"

"What?" Charles was stunned.

"I'm telling you the naked truth. Honest to God, this girl was called Lab, as in 'maabara'—that was her nickname."

"But she told me just the other day that she's still a virgin!"

"She told you she's a virgin? Ha!" the kijana laughed. "Yuyu! Yuhu!" He laughed until his ribs hurt. Charles felt like an idiot. The kijana described Rosa's relationship with the Chancellor. He recounted how Rosa had been on the verge of getting expelled after having an abortion; how she had been in the jaws of death.

"You have to stay alert," the kijana warned him. "Some women are as promiscuous as can be. Yet on their wedding nights, you'll hear their husbands proclaiming that they're virgins! Women like this are using medicine," he explained. "Trust me, I've heard about plenty of women like this. Rosa, too, is going to use medicine on the day of the wedding," he predicted. The young man drained his glass. Charles finished his, as well.

After they parted, Charles went on his way still thinking about the young man's words, but he didn't believe them. He figured that the kijana was just jealous. After two more days had passed, most of the kijana's words seemed downright preposterous. There was just one sentence that was still bothering him: *Rosa is going to use medicine on the day of the wedding.*

Rosa continued visiting Charles just as she had before, and Charles continued to treat her with respect. But the young man who took Charles out for drinks was neither the first nor last kijana to warn Charles of the losses he'd suffer if he married Rosa. Another kijana recounted stories from back when Rosa was a student at Rosary. He recounted how she was expelled from school. He recounted how she had paraded around town with government officials. But because of how much Charles loved and trusted Rosa, all this went in one ear and out the other. Some other words, ones that he thought had some truth to them, he swallowed and endured; he had already made the decision to marry Rosa— his virgin.

If Rosa wasn't really a virgin, it was no fault of his. She was the one who had said it. She was well aware that she had deceived her fiancé. Once you tell a woman that you are going to marry her, she'll start to revere you—so much that she'll no longer give you a preview. If Rosa had allowed him even a taste, she would have wasted her good fortune. Rosa kept her eyes on the prize. She took aim at her prey. If a huntress has only one arrow left, she'll search out a large tree—and if she misses her target, she can climb to safety so she's not eaten alive by the very animal she's hunting. This was exactly what Rosa was doing.

As for Charles? He had wasted much of his life searching for a virgin to marry. As if that wasn't bad enough, he'd propose to prospective partners as soon as he met them. This was exactly what he had done with Rosa. On the very first day, Charles sought engagement. He had written as much in his letter: he had asked for her hand in marriage. Engagement usually comes after a period of friendship, or at least getting to know each other; if engagement comes first, great anxiety is sure to follow.

Rosa clung tightly to her fiancé in the days that followed. She forgot all about Thomas, Deogratias, and the like. Rosa didn't want a long engagement: she was afraid of losing Charles. So during her next visit, she broached the critical question.

"Charles," Rosa began, "I think we've been engaged for long enough now."

"I was just thinking the same thing. I was planning on bringing it up today," Charles assured her. "I'm ready to proceed whenever you are."

"I'd like to get married two months from now," Rosa said.

"A little more time would be better," Charles said. "Give me four months. As you know, Rosa, my parents are very poor," he reminded her. "The more time you give them, the better they'll be able to prepare themselves."

The betrothed couple discussed their wedding plans in great detail. They agreed to go home to see their parents after one more month.

Chapter 12

The intervening month was not a very good one for Rosa. Calamity ensued, calamity after calamity. Just a few days after Charles and Rosa confirmed their marriage plans, a letter appeared on Rosa's desk in the school office. A pen was perched on top of it so it wouldn't blow away. Rosa knew what her missing pen looked like; she was happy to see it again. When she looked at the letter, she saw that it, too, was for her. She opened it. She couldn't believe the words she read. The author of the letter urged Rosa to move out of her room on Uhuru Street as quickly as possible. *Usipohama dada yangu, utakufa baada ya siku mbili,* the letter concluded. If you don't evacuate, sister, you'll be dead within a couple of days.

"Who brought this letter?" Rosa asked the other teachers in the office.

"Some child," one of them answered. "We didn't recognize them."

Rosa was speechless. That day, she didn't teach. She went and reported the threat to the police. She named her nemesis. Rosa's former classmate from Rosary was summoned and told to copy sentences from ten different pages. Her handwriting looked nothing like that of the letter. She was ordered to use her left hand; those samples didn't resemble the letter either. Later on, the police continued their investigation, but there was insufficient evidence; Rosa's case wouldn't stand up in court. Rosa was told she should move, and she was instructed to report to the authorities right away if something similar happened again.

Rosa followed their recommendations. But she had no place to go other than her fiancé's, so she moved in with Charles. Kirumba Street was far from her school, but it was better to live than to die, Rosa figured. She carried on with her work as a teacher. The betrothed couple now slept in the same room, but they were still able to respect one another: each slept in their own bed.

It was almost the time they had promised each other they would go home and see their parents. Charles and his bride-to-be set a date to cross over to the island of Ukerewe, then went to ask permission from the regional education officer. He didn't refuse; the officer granted them one week's leave.

Rosa wrote Flora a lengthy letter. She let Flora know that she had moved, and that she was now living with her fiancé, sparing no effort to heap praise on Charles. *Soon we're going home. Come over on Sunday,* she suggested. Rosa informed Charles that her sister was coming for a visit.

When Flora arrived, she found Charles prepared for the occasion, ready to receive her. She got there at three in the afternoon and needed to get back to where she came from no later than five in the evening. So when she told Rosa how long she had to spend with them, Rosa got right to work fixing her something to eat. While Rosa was preparing the ugali, Charles conversed with Flora.

"What's the news from over there in jela?" he began.

Flora realized that Charles didn't understand properly where she now lived. Nevertheless, she answered him: "Over at the jela everything is just gorgeous."

"Maybe you can tell me something," Charles ventured. "Why do so many more girls get pregnant at your school than at other schools?"

"The main reason, I think," Flora said, "is that we don't have enough freedom. We are watched over, guarded and herded, all the time."

"On this point, I agree with you," Charles said. "You aren't granted sufficient independence. If they're going to watch over you, they could at least watch over you in a way that makes sense. The way they go about it is completely impractical."

"What do you mean when you say watch over us 'in a way that makes sense'?"

"Sensible oversight takes into account someone's actual circumstances—you can't expect someone to sit there forever, next to someone who doesn't resemble them, and not even be allowed to talk to them. Effective oversight requires moderation. Moderate oversight wouldn't prohibit a schoolgirl from talking to boys. These are the very people she's going to live with down the road. I say this," Charles explained, "because we were with a handful of individuals from your school, and all of them seemed to get pregnant within three months. It's as clear as day. If a schoolgirl who's used to being watched over enrolls in a coed institution— like a teachers' training college—she won't be able to handle living among boys. They simply aren't used to each other."

"So what do you think the government should do to prevent schoolgirls from getting pregnant?" Flora asked.

"The government can't prevent pregnancies. It can only limit the schoolgirls' movements. It can't prevent them from getting pregnant across the board," Charles conceded. "When they go back home, for instance?"

"The government says that when we go home," Flora replied, "we're under our parents' supervision."

"So if you get pregnant at home, the government is not at fault?"

"Beyond reproach, they say."

"After watching over you the whole time you're in school!" Charles said in disbelief. "The way I see it, whether or not a schoolgirl gets pregnant depends on how she was brought up when she was much, much younger—that, and her particular circumstances. In addition," Charles continued, "it seems to me that full-grown men are the ones doing most of the impregnating. It's not the schoolgirls' peers—they're just the ones who get blamed most of the time. But even if a schoolgirl gets pregnant by a fellow student, they can still get married. Those important adults, those big men, most of them are already married."

Charles had to put an end to his lecture: Rosa had finished setting the table.

"Karibu mezani," she said to her sister. Flora got up and went to the table, but she refused to eat all by herself. Charles agreed to accompany her; Rosa declined and sat off to the side.

"I heard that a lot of people have died in recent days," Flora started to say.

"Ndiyo," Rosa affirmed. "The other day someone was killed over in Mabatini, and just yesterday someone else was killed right here in Kirumba. Both were murdered for sleeping with other men's wives."

"I think Flora was referring to the five people who died suddenly due to leg sickness," Charles interjected.

"Hapana," Rosa denied. "You didn't understand her. Without a doubt, she meant those people who were killed." Flora, who had in fact been asking about the five, kept quiet.

"This is the downside of Charles," Rosa said. "He prides himself on knowing everything."

"That's your story," Charles rebutted.

"Yes, it is," Rosa said. "Just yesterday you told me that you can read people's thoughts." Charles was silent. Feeling victorious, Rosa went on: "Those murders I mentioned? The police are still investigating them. But the five who died from leg sickness? There's no one following up about that." Charles realized he had better change the subject.

"Shemeji," he said to Flora, already calling her his sister-in-law. "We're going home tomorrow. If you have any messages for those back in Ukerewe, tell them to your sister."

"Rosa already told me you were going in her letter," Flora replied. "I gave her my letters to take home. One is for mama, the other is for Honorata."

"Who's Honorata again?"

"Our sister," Flora reminded him. "The one who comes after me. I bought Emmanuel clothes and a little toy car to play with. Rosa will deliver those, too."

They finished eating. Rosa cleared the dishes from the table. Immediately after washing their hands, Charles brought out a bottle of wine—the Grenado variety.

Charles had a decent amount to drink. Flora drank moderately; she was afraid of getting yelled at when she returned home. Rosa drank with abandon. She was hearkening back to her previous existence; back then, she'd been able to toss back seven bottles of beer in a single sitting. Back then, wine hadn't even had much effect on her. When the first bottle was empty, Charles brought out another one. Rosa finished the second bottle almost entirely on her own. Charles let his fiancée drink to her heart's content.

"Drink up. This is your mji," he told her. Your compound, your home.

"Who's going to cook for you if I get drunk?"

"I'll cook for myself," Charles said.

"Hapana, my darling—hapana," Rosa insisted.

The liquor had taken hold. Rosa rested her head against Charles's chest.

Flora looked at her watch. It was time to leave. "I'm about to get going," she announced.

"Already?" Charles couldn't believe it.

"I have to go," she said. "Haya kwaherini." Okay then—good-bye.

"You're leaving right now?"

"Charles, I have to go."

"Wait a second, I'll see you out," he offered.

"I'm not going anywhere," Rosa said. "Kwaheri. Get home safe."

"Okay, bye," Flora said to her sister. "Give my best to everyone back home."

Charles escorted Flora as far as the bus stop. As luck would have it, a bus came right away. Flora hopped on and headed for town.

She felt satisfied. She had wanted to see the man who was going to marry her sister, and now she'd seen him. She'd found Charles to be polite, hospitable, and a good talker. *But he doesn't surpass my John,* Flora thought. *Also, Charles is a little on the skinny side.*

Once he'd seen Flora off, Charles returned home. He was still somewhat perplexed. He hadn't expected Flora to catch a city-bound bus. He thought she was still a schoolgirl, a student. But Flora had already finished Standard Twelve. After the last day of school, she hadn't gone home to her parents; she'd been picked up by her friend John, who lived at his brother's place in the center of town. This was where Flora currently resided, along with her fiancé. Many people said that Flora was living in sin. Meanwhile, Flora didn't show any signs of getting pregnant. When the results of the Cambridge exam came out, Flora was there at her new home. The results didn't alarm her even a little. She failed; she didn't even get her General Certificate of Education.

"Why should we care when we've already entrusted ourselves to one another?" Flora would say when asked about her exam results. When people warned her, "Soon John's relatives will come to reject you," Flora answered them: "He and I have already discussed it. There's no problem."

Charles was unaware of all of this. He thought Flora was a virgin, just like her sister. When he returned home, he found Rosa in rough shape: she was stretched out on the bed, her eyes closed. Her breathing was barely perceptible. She looked like a corpse.

Charles shook her awake. Rosa opened her eyes for just a moment then shut them again. Charles picked up a book and started to read. Rosa had passed out with one leg thrown to one side and one leg tossed to the other; her sumptuous thighs were on full display. Charles straightened her out and tucked her under the covers. He went back to reading his book.

Everything would have gone smoothly if Charles hadn't

come under Satan's sway. He became overtaken by lust. But it wasn't just lust that made him drop his book to the ground in the middle of reading; it was a wicked notion. Charles recalled the words he'd been told by the kijana. He recalled them exactly:

You have to stay alert. Some women are as promiscuous as can be. Yet on their wedding nights, their husbands proclaim that they're virgins. Women like this are using medicine. Trust me, I've heard about plenty of women like this. It's possible that Rosa, too, will use medicine on the day of the wedding.

The inner workings of Charles's mind began to bother him. He started to think: *Without a doubt, Rosa is wasted right now. I don't suppose she'll be able to tell in the morning. I don't suppose she's in any condition to stop me. This is the time to make sure. Maybe what I'm about to do is wrong. Hapana—Rosa won't know: she's too far gone.* Charles went toward the bed. He heard a voice from within him: *Charles, what you're doing is wrong. You're committing a sin.* His heart began to pound against his chest. Charles kept moving. He reached the bed. He held Rosa. He took her head in his hands and shook it forcefully. "Rosa! Rosa! Amka! Amka! Wake up, time for breakfast!" Rosa was fast asleep. She didn't make a sound. He took hold of her again, this time more gently. She was very drunk. She was completely passed out. He kissed her. Now Charles was in trouble. He began to take off his shoes. He took off his pants. He climbed into the bed and lifted Rosa's dress up as far as her chest. The door and the window were still open; he got up and closed them. He pulled the curtains too. Then he returned to the bed.

Rosa opened her eyes.

Charles froze. "Nisamehe." Forgive me, he said. Rosa let out a very long breath.

"Mmhmm!" she sighed.

Charles panicked. But Rosa didn't open her eyes again. Charles removed her remaining clothes; now Rosa was naked. Charles removed his remaining clothes, as well. His shirt gave him trouble, but he got it off. His undershirt gave him trouble, too.

After some time Charles could be seen wiping the sweat from his body. After wiping off the sweat, he could be seen lifting Rosa from the bed and laying her on the floor. He washed her so she wouldn't be able to tell what had happened while she was drunk. He got a towel and cleaned her thoroughly. He laid her back down on the bed. A rooster crowed, earlier than the usual hour. Charles heard the rooster and glanced at his watch. It was only eleven at night.

Darkness had already fallen when Rosa's "virginity" was taken. Darkness had already fallen when Charles confirmed whether Rosa was really a virgin. Now darkness was spreading out before the betrothed. Charles discovered a huge secret. He saw how the chicken gives eggs, but not milk. A startling realization came over him.

The following morning, Rosa was the first to wake. She came to stretched out on top of the covers, wearing her dress from the night before. Charles was still asleep. Rosa began to wonder how she managed to end up in bed with her clothes on. Then she remembered.

"Charles, Charles!"

"Mmm."

"What time did Flora leave?"

Charles extended his limbs. He flopped his arm over his eyes. "I'm still asleep," he mumbled. "What did you say?"

"What time did Flora leave?" Rosa repeated.

"I walked her out around four-thirty."

Rosa struggled to piece the night back together. "That was some serious liquor," she said. "I've never been so drunk in my life."

"You weren't that drunk," Charles said. "I was drinking along with you."

"Kweli!" said Rosa in disbelief. "I don't remember a thing."

That morning they stayed in bed until eleven o'clock; they were still fatigued from the night before, as if they'd performed arduous labor. In the evening, they began to prepare their things for the journey home.

Chapter 13

It was an awful season in the northern part of Tanzania. Disaster struck all across the region: a new disease of unknown origins had just emerged. The disease was given different names: in Usukumani, people called it "sack disease" because when people fell sick, they tried wrapping their feet in burlap; over in Musoma it was called "funyafunya"; on Ukerewe it was referred to simply as "leg sickness." It was a horrible disease. Someone would be going about in the morning, business as usual, and by evening you would hear that they had passed away. The cause? Leg sickness, you'd be told. Pain began in the chest, then traveled down the back until it reached the knees. A person would lose their strength and drop to the ground—and if they weren't taken to the hospital within two hours, they died. In one day, five or six people might die in a single district. But because death is so universally feared, you'd think that a hundred people had died.

People sought to identify the disease's cause solely through speculation, without testing or examining anything. They said to one another: *We heard that the Frenchman has exploded his bomb over the Sahara. Without a doubt, the bomb has brought about this sickness.* While it was true that the French were up to their experiments in North Africa, this—as doctors pointed out—was not the source of the disease. The disease was said to be some kind of malaria. All this, Charles and his fiancée heard on the ferry heading to Ukerewe.

There on Ukerewe, the disease had everyone on edge. Island children who went to school across the channel, on the mainland, were afraid to come home on holiday; they were afraid of dying. Since Ukerewe is small but densely populated, the sickness spread quickly. In nearly every hamlet, villagers mourned the loss of three or four people each month. The custom of going to an all-night wake eventually had to be adjusted. There were stories of those who went to funerals and died on the spot. When the cause of the disease was eventually discovered, a comprehensive treatment campaign began. Everyone, the healthy and the sick, was given an injection. Every house was sprayed with insecticide. After a while, the disease vanished. People began to say to themselves, *I'll be alive to see another Christmas.*

When Charles and Rosa arrived on the island, the disease was just beginning to spread. Departing from Mwanza, they had already heard of many deaths; even some of their own relatives had died. Charles was devastated when he heard about the death of his uncle Ndalo. Rosa, too, was upset— Ndalo was her family's neighbor. She knew that her mother would be even more upset. She understood that Bigeyo would be most upset of all.

Charles adjusted his travel plans on the spot. Originally, he had planned to go directly to Itira to see his father, but now he would go straight to Namagondo, with Rosa. She was going home, most of all, to see her parents; she looked forward, most of all, to showing them her fiancé. *Surely baba will be happy to see him, and he'll forget all the wrongs I've done him in the past.* These were Rosa's thoughts. For the time being, she wasn't thinking much about Ndalo's death, although it did genuinely upset her.

As Charles approached the compound of his uncle Ndalo—who had died that very morning, of leg sickness—he reached into his bag and withdrew a letter. Charles gave Rosa the letter; but he told her not to read it until that night. "I've described for you the full plan for our engagement and for the day we get married," Charles said, snickering while he said it.

Upon arriving at his aunt and uncle's house, Charles found that the funeral had yet to be performed. It was around two o'clock. He looked upon Ndalo for the last time. After dropping her things at home, Rosa joined Charles at the burial; she had yet to read the letter he had given her. Seated beside her husband's body, Bigeyo sobbed and heaved as she stroked his remains. "Why have you left me behind?" she wailed. "Why didn't you wait for me so we could go together? Kwanini? Why?" Her hair was full of dust. Her breasts were bare.

The grave was prepared, and after being washed, the body was taken outside. Bigeyo threw herself to the ground, crying out: "Kwaheri! Good-bye! I won't see you again!" She followed that with a final word of farewell in the Kerewe language: "Obabwacheyo!" Greet those you meet, wherever you are bound! When the body was lowered into the grave, Bigeyo nearly threw herself down into the hole, on top of it. She had to be restrained. Ndalo was laid to rest. Everyone's eyes were red from crying. Many people had come from across the village to comfort the bereaved, Charles's father among them.

"Ee. You all are still here, watching the days pass. Meanwhile, he's gone and left you all."

"Ee. We're still here. That's the way of the world, isn't it?"

"What can you do, baba? There is no other way."

In this way, the attendees soothed the bereaved. Each of the bereaved was told words such as these and answered with words such as the these. The elders went on the longest. They recounted how the departed was kindhearted, and how he died; they recounted his final words.

Many people had come to pay their respects. The whole compound was filled with sorrow. Right about then, someone could be heard singing a song. The funeral attendees weren't sure, actually, whether it was singing or just a drunkard. When the person in question arrived at the house, all eyes turned to see who it was. The entire compound was silent. It was Zakaria. He swayed from side to side; clearly, he'd been drinking. He began to shout.

"All you who are gathered here, what are you hoping to find? You think this is a wedding? Get out of here already! Ndalo is dead, and tomorrow he'll be rotting! I don't want to hear anyone crying, 'Bwe! Bwe!'"

All the attendees remained quiet. The strangeness of Zakaria's actions could not be overstated. Everyone was astounded: this was not a moment for words such as these. Zakaria was drunk, sure; but it wasn't just drunkenness that made him speak this way; he was accustomed to pointing out the humor in things. Zakaria was someone who was always joking around. He thought he was just playing a prank. When he saw that no one was pleased with his performance, he tried again. He went and climbed on top of Ndalo's grave. Now everyone was watching him in utter shock. Even the women gathered inside the house came out to look at him. Zakaria removed his hat from his head. Perched atop the grave, he began to speak:

"Uhuru wananchi! Wananchi uhuru!" Freedom, countrymen! Countrymen—freedom!

No one responded. Then, a few children broke into giggles. When Zakaria heard them laughing, he continued.

"I, appearing here today in my capacity as chairman of the village drunkards, hereby—" Zakaria's words were cut short; something like a long stick had lodged in his chest. Zakaria fell to his side and died then and there. Just before he toppled over, a woman was heard crying out at the top of her lungs, "Wayii!" The woman's heart stopped; she lay on the ground, dead. A handful of attendees fled the scene, but many stayed. Now someone could be heard boasting, invoking his ancestors.

"In the name of Mkaka and in the name of Kamera! I have slain a dog! A person can't insult someone's household like that and get away with it!"

Zakaria lacked respect. He made an enormous error. But another factor that caused him to say what he did was discovered later on, after he was dead—Zakaria was the villagers' jester. According to the customs of the Wakerewe, a jester can jest at any time and in any place other than a court of law. A jester can also take from his jestees anything not exceeding one goat in value. The jestee must not get angry at this, either. This was how Zakaria pointed out to his neighbors the absurdities of their common existence.

But at that moment, this wasn't yet understood. And so it was that Zakaria lay in a heap atop Ndalo's grave, a spear jutting from his chest. No one thought to go pull it out. Among the women in the crowd, Regina was no longer breathing. She was indeed dead. After a short while, those in the crowd returned to their senses. They removed the spear from Zakaria. When it was taken out, a tremendous amount of blood gushed from his chest. The entire compound reeked of blood.

At the time these calamities occurred, around two hours after Ndalo's funeral ceremony began, Rosa was no longer there. After Ndalo had been laid to rest, Rosa became gripped with anxiety over the letter she'd been given by her fiancé. She rushed home so she could read the letter in private. Before she read the letter, she kissed it. She unfolded the letter carefully, with shaking hands. Finally, she saw what was inside: a small piece of coarse paper, the kind that's used to bag up cement. Rosa didn't believe what she saw. She steadied herself. She read the letter:

So you say you're a virgin, Rosa. Really? Ha! Do you think that after learning how you were passed around in Morogoro, after looking into the chasm with my own two eyes and seeing that ear, do you really think I can still marry you? Ha! Forget it, sister. Not even by force would it be possible! Not even if you were being given away for free!

That was the end of what was written on the little scrap of paper. As soon as Rosa finished reading, her head started to pound. She felt dizzy. Sweat poured from her body. Tears flowed from her eyes down onto her chest. Before, the whole world had been taking mercy on her; now the whole world was laughing at her.

She could not bear to live. To live would be a disgrace.

She searched for a glass bottle. She found one that had hair oil inside—Sperantia's, no doubt. Rosa dumped the oil out; she took the bottle and ground it down into little pieces over a stone. She swept the shards into a glass and added water.

Rosa thought first, before drinking it. She asked forgiveness for her sins. She sought out her finest piece of paper, then sliced her hand open with a razor. With the blood that came out, she wrote some words down on the paper. After she finished writing the words, Rosa summoned her anger. She reflected on her life.

Then, all of a sudden, she drank the water. She lay down on Honorata's bed. Right away, blood began to flow from her mouth. The shards of glass had lacerated her throat. Rosa spat and saw blood, "Asante. Kifo njoo upesi." Thank you, she said. Death, come quickly. After a little while, she felt a very sharp pain in her stomach. It wasn't long before Rosa realized she was beginning to lose consciousness. She started to see something like smoke in front of her eyes. She uttered her final words. No one heard them except the hornets that had built their nest in the rafters.

"I am dying; now I am truly dying. My life was a difficult one. It's clear now that the source of my misery was my upbringing. Malezi. Upbringing. Not how my mother raised me, but how my father did. Baba really watched over me. I was watched like those schoolgirls stuck in jela. When I gained my independence, I failed to use my freedom. Deogratias, Thomas, Charles—I lost them all." Rosa said good-bye to her siblings. "Kwaheri Flora, kwaheri Honorata, kwaheri Stella, kwaheri Sperantia, Emmanuel kwaheri!" Then she bid farewell to her father and mother: "Baba na mama," she said, "I'm sorry if I've done wrong."

She started to see twinkling lights: stars. She screamed. "A priest! I see a priest! What are you reading? Biblia? Padri? Don't go! Wait! Tell me more!"

Rosa could say no more; her eyes had closed. When Honorata arrived to tell her the news of her parents' deaths, she thought Rosa was asleep. "Rosa! Rosa!" she said.

Rosa didn't move.

"Rosa! Wake up, baba and mama have died!" Rosa didn't move.

"Rosa!" she cried. "Can't you hear me?"

Rosa was still. Honorata realized that Rosa wasn't breathing. She was dead: her body cold to the touch. Honorata fainted and fell to the floor.

Shortly thereafter, the bodies of Zakaria and Regina were brought to the house so they could be laid out. It was going to be difficult to have a funeral for them that same day. Many people hadn't made it back to their own homes since the morning. They were getting hungry. In addition, the funeral rites couldn't be performed before the relatives of the deceased were all gathered; Flora had yet to arrive. Some people present wanted the funeral done that day. They said, "Since their firstborn is present, we can bury them today— so tomorrow, we can get back to our responsibilities." They didn't yet know where Rosa was; no one had seen her after Ndalo's funeral.

The neighbors were still debating what to do when they heard Stella wailing as she emerged from the house. Instead of crying out the names of her father and mother, she was crying out the names of Rosa and Honorata. People ran into the house to see what had happened. Rosa was stretched out on the bed, dead. Honorata was stretched out down below;

she was still breathing, albeit faintly. When they checked her pulse, they found her blood was still circulating. Honorata was carried outside so she could get some fresh air. Water was poured on her, to try to bring her back to consciousness.

Never before had the village of Namagondo seen such a catastrophe. Four dead in a single day! All of them neighbors! And three of them from the same household! The entire village was saturated with sadness. Those who had intended to go home stayed in order to see if Honorata would be okay. Others, from the outskirts of the village, came to look upon the bodies. When the herders heard the news, they left their cattle in the pastures and came running; they had to see it to believe it. The women who had left to fetch water were dumbfounded when they heard what had transpired in their absence. Their calabashes, crocks, and jerry cans full of water fell from atop their heads. They cried out together in disbelief: "Wuuu!" The cows that had been left out to graze roamed recklessly. They ate cassava; they ate marando; they ate rice plants; there was no one to watch over them. Everyone was at Zakaria's house.

Later that night, Honorata came to. The villagers saw that she was going to be okay. They laid out the three corpses in a row and returned to their respective homes to search for something to put in their stomachs. The night was strangely peaceful. The whole village felt sorrow for the four girls and their brother who were left. Even the youngest children of the village detected that something had happened that day. They, too, were saddened. Some children asked their fathers, "How come everyone is so quiet?" No one answered. Others asked, "Didn't Maji Machafu have anything to drink today? We haven't heard him singing!" No one could answer that question, either. Zakaria's drinking mates were utterly depressed. There was no one to howl at the moon that night. When Zakaria was drunk, he sang and hollered, *Hoi, Hoi!* Practically the entire village was accustomed to hearing his voice, but that night, no voice could be heard. Zakaria was dead. People were amazed. "Jamani," they said, "death hangs over us! Maji Machafu"—Dirty Water—"is among the deceased. Truly, death hangs over us!" Even those who weren't related to Zakaria were upset. In the dead of the night, owls' screeches tore through the village. Children cowered in their beds. People of the island believe that if an owl screeches near someone's compound, death descends on someone within. The owls cried out through the night; fear increased.

For the wake, Rosa was laid out on one side of the room and Zakaria was laid out on the other. Regina was laid out between them. This was how their bodies were arranged. A light stayed on in the room through the night. Off to the side, Stella and Sperantia could be seen weeping. Emmanuel also shed tears; for the time being, he cried because his sisters were crying. The anguish of losing his father, mother, and sister was beyond his grasp. The children kept vigil together while they cried. They wept for their parents; they wept for their sister.

The heads of the deceased were left uncovered, so the children could look upon their parents one last time. Zakaria's face showed clearly that he had been in agony when he died. Regina's face was at rest, peaceful. She looked healthy, even in death. Rosa's face seemed to contain a smile. Although she was in pain when she died, she had been able to close her mouth and shut her eyes. Truly, these three faces had something to tell the world. The trio of faces held important secrets—the secret to life, the secret to love, and the secret to upbringing.

The following morning, those who looked at Rosa's face said, "I've never seen a girl who suffered in life quite like this one!" Those who looked at Regina's face said, "Never in my life have I seen a woman who loved her children quite like this one!" Those who looked at Zakaria's face remarked, "The bruiser really knew how to booze it up. There's no one who watched over his daughters quite like him!"

The bodies were washed before the burial. The corpse washers found a little piece of paper tucked into Rosa's armpit. It was a very high-quality piece of paper onto which words had been written in blood. Across the top was the name "Charles." They read:

Charles—I loved you. I love you even now. Charles, it's for your sake that I'm killing myself. But because I love you, I'll tell you an important secret you should take to heart. Charles, marrying a virgin happens only by chance; it's not something to search for—and if you sample your bride before getting married, she's not a virgin anymore, even if she was before.

Charles was right outside. He was called in and given the letter. As soon as he finished reading, he looked at Rosa. He longed for her to be his wife; but now she was dead. He left.

Three graves were dug in the section of the cemetery reserved for the faithful. Flora was telephoned. It was announced that the funeral would be performed at one o'clock, after the ferry arrived from Mwanza. They were waiting for Flora, since she now was the one who remained to take care of her younger siblings. Flora arrived by airplane, along with her fiancé. When she heard of all the disasters, she fainted, but soon she returned to her senses. Because she arrived at nine in the morning, the funeral was moved forward an hour. Most of the relatives of the deceased were already present. The priest arrived at the village church at twelve noon and donned his frock. He sprinkled holy water over the bodies, which had been laid out earlier. "If you kept a record of sin," he began, "who among us—ee Bwana—could stand upright?"

Psalms were read. After a short while, the priest read a prayer.

"We ask you, ee Bwana, to pardon the souls of your servants, Rosa, Regina, and Zakaria, for their offenses, so that after passing from this world they may reside in your kingdom. And for how they erred in their lives owing to weakness of the flesh, absolve them with your gentleness and your compassion. In the name of Christ, our Lord."

Everyone ended the prayer together: "Amina."

Another psalm was read. The church service concluded, and the bodies were carried to the cemetery. A crowd had gathered. Charles was among those awaiting the burials. The village drunkards were present, too; they had come to see their friend laid to rest. When the priest arrived at the cemetery, he blessed the graves. After singing a few hymns, he read another prayer, a longer one. Charles was shaking: he thought perhaps his name too had been written into it, close to the Devil's.

"Ee Mungu, all your creations live in you," the priest began. "And when our bodies die, they aren't lost to you, but rather transformed into something greater. So we implore you, with your kindness and sympathy, have mercy on your servants' souls and wipe away the sins that befell them when they failed to fulfill your love because of Satan's machinations, and their own weakness and wickedness." (No one added, *or as a result of poor upbringing.*) "Command the angels . . ."

The priest had yet to conclude when someone shouted: "I brought Zakaria two bottles of moonshine. He should drink one as a farewell to us drunkards! The second he'll take with him to the Kingdom of Christ. Amina!" Everyone was stunned. The weak among them giggled. People thought it was some kind of skit. The man took one bottle and tossed it onto Zakaria's grave. He was picked up and taken home.

The priest continued with the service. The bodies were lowered into their graves. Regina's grave was in the middle. Her husband was on her right and her daughter was on her left. After they were in their graves, the priest took a shovel and tossed a little bit of dirt into each one. Then the relatives of the deceased did the same. The stronger members of the crowd filled in the graves in a hurry. Many shovels were at work. When Honorata saw people dumping dirt into the graves with no sympathy whatsoever, when she heard the soil cascading down onto her parents and sister, she fainted again. She was picked up and carried home.

The graves were filled. Now that the funeral was complete, the women began crying all over again. Flora wailed. She cried very, very loudly. She lay down on top of her mother's grave, rolled from side to side. Some women had to grab her to stop her from thrashing. Unable to walk on her own, Flora was supported between two women and escorted home. On the way, she wailed, "Yoho yoo wai! It's not possible! This isn't possible!"

Honorata, Stella, and Sperantia—all their eyes were blood-shot from crying.

Back at the compound, many people had gathered. The women of the village understood the difficulties facing the young children who'd been left on their own. Nearly every woman in Namagondo brought over a basin of flour that evening. The men brought firewood. John contributed a certain amount of money; others were sent to go buy fish. When night fell, the crowd dispersed, and people went home to sleep. Only the relatives of the deceased remained, and those who were close to them. That night it poured. Or-dinarily, those attending a wake spend the night outside, but on this night they sought shelter. Only one person spent the night outdoors—Honorata. Rain beat against her body.

The following three days were days of mourning. Be-fore she died, the late Regina had built her cattle stock back up to four cows. After all the prepared dishes that had been brought to the wake were gone, the extended family ordered that Regina's cows be slaughtered, so people could continue to eat. The cows were slaughtered, one each day. Although this kind of mourning usually lasts three days, everyone stayed on for a fourth day, when the final cow was slaugh-tered. The following two days were devoted to drinking. Everyone drank away. You would think there had been no tragedy. When the meat was gone, the relatives scattered. Some didn't even say good-bye. Other family members re-mained to divide up the estate. It was well known that Za-karia had seven hundred shillings in the bank, set aside for Emmanuel. The relatives forced Flora to withdraw the money from the bank so they could divide it up. But when Flora went to the bank, she was unable to withdraw the funds. Her relatives nearly went insane. They called her a thief, a malaya, an mshenzi. The relatives realized that this was a women's compound.

But Zakaria was once a teacher. He knew that problems would occur regarding the inheritance of his estate. After failing to find the keys to open Zakaria's locked chests of valuables, the relatives smashed them apart with an axe. In one box, they found fifty shillings in an envelope with Regina's name written on it. In another, they found a tiny document that described in full who was to inherit what: his will. Zakaria had written it years before. Religious leaders were present to see that it abided by legitimate rights of possession. The document stated that Zakaria's only heirs were his children; each child had been designated certain assets to inherit. The relatives refused to believe that the will was in Zakaria's own handwriting. When the religious leaders pushed back, the relatives chased them away with pangas. Now they were free to do what they pleased.

The relatives got their inheritances, all right. They reaped and reaped, dividing up all Zakaria's possessions. They inherited everything left in his house. They inherited his orange and mango trees. They inherited his banana plants. They inherited his cats and dogs. They inherited his mats of dried grass that served as his roofing material, and the wooden posts that enabled his house to stand. They inherited his farms and fields. They inherited his hens; they even inherited his cow manure. They inherited. Those relatives, they truly inherited. Yet there wasn't a person among them who said they'd take responsibility for one of the orphaned children. Instead, they demanded that John pay a dowry, so they could divide that up, too. Rosa's things went on to be taken as well.

After the divvying-up was done, the children stayed in

the house for just one more day. Every time they touched something, they were told it wasn't theirs. "Your money is in the bank," their relatives reassured them. Flora asked the nuns in Kagunguli to help her care for her younger siblings for a period of two years. They didn't refuse: they took pity on her. The next day, Honorata, Stella, Sperantia, and Emmanuel were all taken to Kagunguli. Together with John, Flora began the journey back to Mwanza. The adversities they had been through together made John truly love Flora. Compassion caused them to love each other as never before. While still at the house in Namagondo, John took Flora in his arms and promised her, "Flora, I will provide for you; and after two more years at my job, I will provide for your younger siblings."

Flora told those who claimed to be her kin: "John's not going to shell out a single banknote to you people. To provide for my sisters and brother—no mahari could be greater than that!" They set off on their journey to Mwanza and lived like husband and wife.

Back on the island, Flora's relatives knocked down the house and scavenged the roofing material along with the wooden posts. When the oranges ripened, they came and plucked them too. They even farmed Zakaria and Regina's fields. As for Bigeyo? She returned to where she was from. She, too, inherited nothing; everything was taken by Ndalo's relatives. That marked the end of these two households that had so much to tell the world.

Charles, after receiving that little letter written in blood, was troubled by pangs of conscience. There was truth in the letter's words, he sensed. Relying on chance had been good for nothing. He had been unable to find a virgin, even though a virgin was what he craved. A few days after Rosa's funeral, Charles went to Kisubi and joined the monastery. He chose a life of celibacy, far on the other side of the lake.

*   *   *

One day, while living in Kagunguli, Honorata walked to the village of Namagondo—a distance of around seven miles. Stella and Sperantia accompanied her. They arrived at the cemetery where Rosa and their parents were buried. They planted an orange tree at the head of each grave so they wouldn't lose track of where they were.

The trees sprouted successfully and didn't delay in growing. But as they matured, only one tree bore good fruit—the tree that was in the middle. The two trees on either side bore fruit that was inedible. Even after ten years, as soon as it was orange season, the children would cross over from Mwanza to harvest fruit from that tree in the middle. They consumed their mother's body and they consumed their mother's blood. They remembered their mother.

Later on, when they were all grown up, Emmanuel recounted to his sisters this dream that he had dreamt long ago, while he was asleep.

The Case of Rosa Mistika

MUNGU (GOD) is seated atop his royal throne, wearing enormous spectacles. A MALAIKA (ANGEL) passes carrying a stiff piece of paper on which is written "The Case of Rosa Mistika."

MUNGU: Rosa, why have you killed yourself?

ROSA: Ah, Mungu. All this has transpired because of my father.

ZAKARIA enters. He has a dark mark on his chest. He bows down before MUNGU.

MUNGU: I will ask you again, Rosa. Why have you killed yourself?

ROSA: Ah, Mungu. All this has transpired because of my father.

MUNGU: Zakaria, what do you have to say in your defense?

ZAKARIA: Ah, Mungu. All this has transpired because of her own weakness and wickedness.

MUNGU: Do you have any evidence, Rosa?

ROSA: Yes, Bwana. The whole world.

MUNGU: *(Turning to ZAKARIA)* And you, Zakaria?

ZAKARIA: The whole world, Mungu my Lord.

MUNGU stands up. He removes his spectacles. He reflects. He points at ROSA.

MUNGU: Truly, you are a Rosa Mistika. *MUNGU points down below.* I will ask the people!

MUNGU exits; thunder sounds.

Translator's Acknowledgments

It has been a tremendous honor, daunting challenge, and ongoing pleasure to attempt to translate the language, feeling, concepts, and world of Euphrase Kezilahabi's *Rosa Mistika*. The English version is not the Swahili one, and many differences between the two were inevitable from the outset. Although the responsibility for any shortcomings is ultimately my own, for the translation's successes I have a great many individuals and organizations to thank, all the more so because of my long relationship to the novel.

For introducing me to *Rosa Mistika* and to the figure of Kezilahabi as an undergraduate Swahili student (and for introducing me to Swahili), I thank Professor F.E.M.K. Senkoro. For facilitating the Intensive Summer Swahili program at the University of Dar es Salaam, I thank Professor Aldin Mutembei. For teaching me in that program, and for so much more, I thank Dr. Fokas Nchimbi.

For responding to my earliest inquiries about translating *Rosa Mistika,* I thank Annmarie Drury, Katriina Ranne, and Catherine Shoni. I also must acknowledge the early and invaluable support of the 2022 PEN/Heim Translation Fund Grant that I was awarded. Shortly thereafter followed my introduction to Kelsey McFaul—thanks, Kelsey, for your ongoing interest in and support of my work as a translator. I'd also like to thank Abdulrazak Gurnah. I was immersed in his novels while doing my early passes; they contain many rich examples of how to convey various senses of Swahiliness in literary English. Asante.

For picking out of the slush pile the excerpt from chapter 3 that went on to be published in *Northwest Review,* I thank S. Tremaine Nelson. Later on, the *Hopkins Review* published chapter 7 in its entirety. For that publication, I thank Dora Malech and Phoebe Oathout for their support and excellent editorial work.

I have many thanks and thanks of different kinds for writers and translators who were and are part of the Queens College MFA Program in Creative Writing and Literary Translation. I began my translation as part of my application to the program, completed my first draft while in the program, and revised the manuscript and wrote about process as part of my thesis project. Thanks to Nicole Cooley, Annmarie Drury, and Roger Sedarat for facilitating the workshops where *Rosa Mistika* was read and discussed. Thanks to all my workshopmates for their many helpful suggestions and insightful comments. Among my fellow students, special thanks to Richard Prins, also a literary translator from Swahili, for his close, comparative readings and countless invaluable contributions. Thanks also to visiting professor Crystal Hana Kim, for her brilliant course on multilingual texts. For his amazing comments, and for showing me how a reader not bilingual in Swahili and English is capable of responding to the many *mafumbo* posed by Kezilahabi, thanks to Jeff Cassvan. Special thanks are also due to Rebecca Suzuki, for her brave, inspiring approach to literary translation and all it can encompass.

Many other writers, translators, and scholars supported me during my translation of *Rosa Mistika,* both by offering helpful feedback on the translation itself and in ways less direct. They include but are by no means limited to Noemi Adrigeri, Meg Arenberg, Roberto Gaudioso, Ida Hadjivayanis, E. J. Koh, Idza Luhumyo, Esther Karin Mngodo, Fadhy Mtanga, Makafane Tšepang Ntlamelle, and Terese Svoboda (who has been a creative writing mentor, across genres, for many years). Friends in Tanzania were also available for consultation at a moment's notice: asanteni sana Nangu Mpinga na Anthony Safari Sarota.

At Dar es Salaam University Press, many, many thanks to Dr. Aman Mdewa, Rahma Muhdhar, and Catherine Shoni for their trust, graciousness, and willingness to work with me—thank you to everyone at DUP whom I met with in person in June 2023. Enormous gratitude is also due to the family of the late Professor Euphrase Kezilahabi. Particular thanks to George Kezilahabi and to Florida Kezilahabi, for their warmth, humor, hospitality and for trusting me to represent Euphrase Kezilahabi to the English-speaking world. Shukrani za dhati.

At Yale University Press, I thank Abbie Storch for her early interest in the novel, which has grown into a boundless enthusiasm. Thank you for navigating this entire process with me, for your astute editorial work, for your belief in Kezilahabi's voice and story, and for your belief in my abilities as a translator. Thanks also to Ann-Marie Imbornoni for shepherding this project through the production process, and to Ann Twombly for her invaluable copyediting skills.

These thanks would be incomplete if I failed to loop back to two individuals: Dr. Fokas Nchimbi and Annmarie Drury. Dr. Nchimbi is not just a former Swahili instructor of mine, but a dear friend and mentor, and someone who read every word of my translation in its earliest version, paying particular attention to fidelity to the source language. As you said when we met again, face to face, after over a decade: "Utimilifu wa wakati." The fullness of time.

Annmarie Drury's talents as a translator, poet, editor, scholar, and teacher are matched by and very much related to her endless thoughtfulness, unusual patience, and loving heart. Annmarie was an early point of contact for me at Queens College, my workshop instructor, and my thesis advisor. She also worked directly with Euphrase Kezilahabi on her stunning translations of his poetry. In that sense, she is a vital link to what Kezilahabi's voice sounds like in English. At the same time, Annmarie encouraged me to search for my own version of Kezilahabi's voice, and to do so while being evermore aware of the qualities that make his voice unique in Swahili.

I must also mention the "women's compound" scene in chapter 3. What my version of it ended up being was directly influenced by Annmarie Drury's translation of the same passage, which she incorporated into "Searching for Swahili Jane," her contribution to the translation studies book *Prismatic Jane Eyre.* I was initially struck by Annmarie's insight into the foreshadowing contained in this passage; after reading her words, I became convinced that my rendering of "mji wa wanawake" as "a compound without a man around to guard it" was no longer either tenable or desirable. It became "a women's compound," as it should have been all along. Though this was the primary change I intended to make, I ended up letting Annmarie's translation guide me in its diction throughout the passage. What I settled on is a blend of her translation and my own, and for that I must both acknowledge her labors as a translator and recommend her beautiful contribution to *Prismatic Jane Eyre.* I also acknowledge drawing on some of Annmarie's translation choices in *Stray Truths,* the selection of Kezilahabi's groundbreaking poetry that she translated and edited, which is also highly recommended. Thank you sincerely, Annmarie, for all of this, and for the many other kinds of assistance and encouragement you have given me—the contextualizing foreword that you agreed to author is just the latest perfectly timed example. Asante sana.

I also thank Euphrase Kezilahabi, of course—not just for *Rosa Mistika* and for his other works, but for the part of him that lives on in the world and continues to create.

Finally, taking a cue from Kezilahabi's own dedication: *How can a person ever thank their mother enough for the kindness she showed them when they were still a little child?* For encouraging me in my linguistic and literary endeavors for longer than I can remember, thanks to my mother, Suzie Boss; to my father, Bruce Rubin; and to my brother, Daniel Rubin. Thanks also to that other member of my family, Miriam Latzer, for your love and support that, literally and figuratively, has traveled all over the world.

Jay Boss Rubin

EUPHRASE KEZILAHABI (1944–2020) was a Tanzanian fiction writer, poet, dramatist, philosopher, and scholar. One of the most celebrated Swahili authors of the twentieth and twenty-first centuries, he wrote six novels that range in style from social realism to experiments in postmodernism. He was among the very first Swahili writers to publish poetry in free verse, a provocation that divided Swahili poets in the 1970s but has since been embraced by many as a necessary renovation. Kezilahabi was born and raised in the village of Namagondo, on Ukerewe Island in Lake Victoria. He received his bachelor's and master's degrees from the University of Dar es Salaam, and a PhD from the University of Wisconsin–Madison. His body of work—singular, existential, humorous, complex—is characterized by the exploration of abstract ideas through everyday language. In 1995 he joined the faculty of the Department of African Languages and Literature at the University of Botswana, and he continued to teach there until shortly before his passing away. *Rosa Mistika,* Kezilahabi's first novel, as well as his first to be published in full in its English translation, was originally published in 1971.

JAY BOSS RUBIN is a translator and writer from Portland, Oregon. He received his MFA in Creative Writing and Literary Translation from Queens College, City University of New York, and was a recipient of a 2022 PEN/Heim Translation Fund Grant to enable the completion of his translation of *Rosa Mistika.* His Swahili–English translations have been published by Two Lines Press, *The Common, Asymptote, Hopkins Review,* and *Northwest Review,* among other outlets.